SOMEONE SAVAGE

MIKE MCCRARY

BAD
WORDS INC.

SOMEONE SAVAGE

MIKE MCCRARY

SOMEONE SAVAGE

MIKE McCRARY

It's better to be good than evil, but one achieves goodness at a terrific cost. - Stephen King

PART ONE

PART ONE

ONE

FEW PEOPLE LIVE after meeting Edward Frakes.

The rare few who've lived long enough to talk about the meeting can be counted on the tips of a person's fingers. Been times when they could be counted on one hand.

Frakes has stopped a lot of heartbeats. A special brand of violence that erases unwanted relationships before they can begin. He's also broken the lives of others he's never met or ever will meet.

Two of the few still breathing are here, only a few feet from Frakes, huddled inside a small, rusted metal shed nestled amongst the trees. A sprawl of mountains just outside its locked door framed under the moonlight.

Frakes presses his ear to the shed.

Impatience makes his skin crawl like a thousand ants under his flesh. Racing along his bones. Maybe he hears them breathing inside the shed, maybe he doesn't. Hard to parse those delicate sounds from the night noise that hums throughout the woods surrounding him. The whispering of the trees, the soft symphony of katydids and crickets swallows his senses whole. This place at night can trick a man into hearing all kinds of things.

Wait.

Is that...

Are they laughing at me inside there?

A pulse of anger thumps. He slaps the shed. The metal rattles and creaks before settling back into the quiet harmony of the night. Doesn't realize he did it until his hand drops back down by his side. Sometimes the anger pulse makes him act before his thoughts can register as rational.

"You done?" He pounds his meaty hand hard on the shed door. "Learn your lesson in there?"

Stepping back, he waits. His darting, smallish eyes—perhaps only small compared to rest of his hulking skull—scan the stars that pepper the night sky.

A cool breeze drifts across his large frame,

blowing what little hair he has left. Trees that seemingly stretch a mile high swaying like slow metronomes keeping time with the evening's soothing rhythm. He breathes in the smell of the trees. Maybe pines and ash, Frakes isn't sure. Mama would know things like that. There's a kind of calm to this place. A peace that resides here in the woods at night, if only Frakes could let some of that calming peace inside his mind.

There's a way to peace if you can simply let it in, someone once told him.

Or maybe it was in a movie or he heard it on one of those television shows Mama likes so much. Religious preachy-prose-bullshit, maybe? Frakes shakes his head hard. Those thick thoughts drop down, dipping into the darkness. Falling into that cold, pitch-black pit dug into his brain where he oddly finds the most comfort.

"You hearin' me?" Spit flies.

Rage accessed in a snap. Always near. Never drifting, never leaving.

The metal shed shudders and shakes as he beats harder on the door. The whole thing could bust apart any second, sending sheets of metal to the ground if he keeps at it too long. Chunky confetti the color of dried-blood brown falls off the door as he slaps the shed with his fat palm again and again. Stopping, peeling back away from the frail structure, Frakes sucks in a deep breath searching for the strength to find some of that calm. He squeezes his fists tight, then tighter, until he feels his fingernails dig into his skin, then releases them quick. Repeats. Fighting to dull the pulse.

It's quiet inside the shed, but he can hear them moving now.

The sounds of quick, frightened breathing are now unmistakable.

Disgusted with himself, he shakes his head, remembering they won't answer him no matter how hard he slams his stupid hand against the metal. One of them doesn't talk at all and the other one usually only speaks in one-word responses. Three words max. Can't believe he forgot those things about them. His mind, it's been cloudy lately. There's been a smoothing to the edges he used to have. The sharpness he needs in this life. Mama's voice starts banging around inside his head. Her gravel-and-gravy voice pours her lifetime chant over his brain.

Stupid.

Stupid.

Stupid Eddie Frakes.

Turning his head to look back, as if on cue Mama stands a few feet behind him.

"They're just gonna try that shit again." Mama snuffs out her cigarette into the dirt and flips a fresh one between her lips. "But you better let 'em out. Don't want a bigger mess than you've already done."

His head dips down. A massive man made small.

She fires up her fresh smoke with what could best be called a handheld propane torch. Mama has supper ready. Frakes can smell it through the open door to the main house. It's waiting for him. Waiting for everyone. Her cooking is like home. A shitty home, he knows, but home nonetheless.

Frakes looks back to the shed.

Knuckles pop. He knows his appearance frightens them but there's not much he can do about that. His thick hands are marked with scars from struggles won and lost. A fat pinkish scar runs from below his left eye to his throat. Care of a near-death experience a couple of years ago. A complete death experience for the other fella. Frakes keys the lock and yanks the door open. The door creaks with a metallic wail.

Two children sit huddled on a torn blanket.

The girl is eight. The boy is seven.

7

They hold one another, then release quick. The moonlight cuts a faint shaft of light through the open doorway. Their eyes are hard. Much harder than they should be at this age. Faces blank. Their small bodies vibrate at the sight of him as if they are holding back, not wanting to show him how scared they truly are.

Frakes stands outside, his head tucked down, keeping his face in the shadows. He thumbs back toward the house. A silent instruction that it's time to come inside. Mama huffs, turning away and walking back into the house through the back door.

The house is dark save for a few candles and a light with a bright-colored, daisy-decorated shade that hangs above a busted-up table. Dirty pots and pans are piled high in the sink. Plastic yellow plates with half-eaten meals have cemented themselves to the surface of the kitchen counter. Mama takes a seat amongst the filth, smoking like a chimney. She opens her arms wide in half-hearted, half-assed attempt to seem welcoming. Smile broken and false.

There are four plates set out with forks and spoons waiting.

The boy and the girl shake their heads, refusing to come inside.

"Come on now." Frakes talks slow and thick, like he's speaking with a mouthful of Jell-O.

He slips from the shadows into the moonlight. There's a spray of crimson across his face. Almost completely dry and starting to flake. He offers his one uncovered hand to them, still holding the lock to the shed. Hopes they'll come out and join them for supper without him having to be mean about it. A rubber glove covers his other hand. The thick blue glove is pulled up to his elbow, slick and shiny with blood that looks dark purple in the moonlight.

"Been working all damn day," Frakes says. "Tired. Hungry as hell. Sure you'd appreciate a bite to eat too."

He looks to the children.

The children stare back. Giving him nothing.

Booming silence.

"Alright then." Frakes begins to shut the door, shaking the lock back and forth for them to see.

"No," the girl says. There's no begging in her voice. A command, not a request.

"*No?*" Frakes's eyebrows raise his chubby face. He rubs the scraps of facial hair he likes to think of as a beard. "Any chance you two littles can be good? Friendly, even?"

"No." Not an ounce of fear in her two-letter response.

The girl tosses a cheap, plastic cell phone at his feet. One of those kid cell phones—they call them dumb phones—that can only talk or text with one number. Frakes's number. He couldn't completely turn off access to emergency numbers like 911 and so on, but he made it borderline impossible to make that call using this phone. Buried deep in the settings is a feature designed to keep a kid from misdialing 911 by accident.

On the screen is a series of missed calls and texts. All from Frakes. He'd made her take the phone after the last time they misbehaved. Thought he might communicate with the littles from the house. Make his life easier. Didn't work.

Frakes smiles. Can't help it.

"Suppose *friendly* is a lot to ask." Frakes looks back to Mama. She shrugs. He knows she's growing impatient too. Supper getting cold and all. Turning back to the boy and girl, he says, "You gotta eat, so I'll tell you what, then. As a peace offering—or something—Mama here is going to bring you a plate to share."

Mama rolls her eyes, then picks up a plate from the table and starts spooning something steamy from the stove.

"That work?"

The girl and boy offer only a stare in response to the proposed bargain.

Mama moves out from the kitchen like a cannonball, steaming plate of mush and a glass of water in her hands. Doesn't bother with the utensils.

Frakes steps away from the door as Mama delivers the meal to the shed's dirty floor, then rushes back to the house. He knows the boy and girl will come around. Been through this before. Last night, even. They're tough but not superheroes.

His mind shifts back to his work.

Closes his eyes tight. Punches his thigh hard. Upset that he forgot something. Distracted by this situation with the boy and girl. Mama is getting into his head too. Making him forget the details, and the devil that lies in those details. He's already made mistakes, can't keep making them. His face flushes red. Heartbeat rises. Everything, all of the time, inside his head.

Frakes needs to finish up with a mess from work. The mess sitting in the trunk of his car. Frakes did good today, did some good work, but he needs to finish up. Those men from the job this morning are dead as the dodo, sure, but they still require his attention. Two men he was told to take care of. Was told to make go away.

All the way gone, is what was said.

What's left of both of them is still resting in his trunk. Frakes knows he needs to do what he's told. Never half-asses a job—*Full-on Frakes* they call him sometimes—but those dead men will have to wait until after supper. Mama will be mad if she has to wait a single minute more.

Battles gotta be chosen in this life.

"Damn." Frakes grunts as he locks the shed door.

TWO

"AMAZING, RIGHT?"

Grace Jennings slow-waves her presenting arm, showing off the perfectly framed view of the scenic mountains and endless sea of trees.

"All this and still only an hour and a half drive to New York. Philadelphia too. Hard to imagine being this secluded yet still so close to all the crazy of the city, right? Did you just drive in this morning?"

Nicholas Hooper had asked people around New York for some references to help him find a place to rent out here. Grace Jennings was the name that popped up as the top real estate agent in the Poconos.

A few people at Hooper's publisher had worked with her on their vacation homes and such. He talked to her twice on the phone. She did most of the talking, actually—he listened, or pretended to—but he liked most of what he heard. He knew the in-person appointment was going to be a much bigger show.

Pushing his round, wire-framed glasses up, Hooper gives a half-smile with some fake-attention nods as he rides the rolling waves of her pitch. The glasses have become a bit of a trademark for the author. Hooper likes to think they give him a young John Lennon appeal. His sister says it's more like an old-ass Harry Potter. Not a bad thing, Hooper loves the books and the films, but still not the same as the musical voice of the universe.

Grace keeps on at selling the place, unaware of the mental distance between Hooper and her flawless pitch. Hooper's instructions about what he wanted in a house were simple but specific. As he drove up to the place, he knew Grace had done her job well. No matter how painful listening to her over-the-top spiel was going to be.

This place just might do.

There's a long, tall mirror off the living room near the front door. Hooper catches a look at himself as they walk in. Didn't realize the change in his appearance until now, but he hasn't really looked at himself lately.

Is that possible? Or have I just not paid attention?

Either way, he's looking himself over now and can't help but notice the weight loss. They said that would happen. Fighting back a smile, he thinks about how he can get back on the carbs now that this unsolicited diet plan is upon him. Pros and cons to everything, he supposes.

"Used to be an inn, did I tell you that already? This huge property used to be a bed and breakfast too. Now, it's been converted to an amazing rental opportunity. Total of eight bedrooms and eight and a half baths, three bedrooms on the first floor, five bedrooms upstairs. There's a lovely little library space. Great deck off the master." Grace stops. Thinks, looking Hooper over. "Are you planning on entertaining often. Family? Friends?"

"No." Hooper sips his coffee. Found a local place not too far away in the tiny town nearby that makes a damn nice cup of coffee. That's important to Hooper. "Not really the entertaining sort of dude."

"Oh. I mean it's such a big place. I thought maybe—"

"Well, my sister will probably be coming and going. If she can stand me and my *mountains of shit*, as she lovingly phrases it. Most of the time it will only be me and my gorgeous, broken brain."

Why can't I talk like a human being to other human beings?

Hurts to hear myself speak sometimes.

Hooper almost breaks his eyes trying to keep them from rolling. He pulls off his skull cap and rubs his fresh buzz cut. Still working on getting used to it. Only fuzz, really, cut so close to the scalp. Grace nods, keeping her big, fake smile turned on full blast. A pro no matter who or what comes her way.

Hooper gets lost for a moment in her bright, lifeless, always-be-closing eyes.

Thoughts plume into a mushroom cloud. Thoughts of why he came here. He's planned a lot. Not his strong suit, but he does have a plan. Wrote some of it down. Not an elegant plan by any stretch, but it's what he's got. Playing out a situation he never asked for.

Blinking, smiling back, Hooper holds on loosely to the delicate art of being pleasant while waiting for a conversation to lose steam. He's already made up his mind on this place but doesn't want to rob Grace of her moment to shine him on with her skills. She seems to love it. It's obvious she's run through this routine many, many times in her professional life, but she does have a certain natural flare that's hard to walk away from.

Hooper resets.

Knows he doesn't owe her an explanation for why he's renting this massive home for only himself, but for some reason, he feels he needs to try again. His mother always pushed hard on having manners and giving respectful responses to everyone. Even with his mother's sharp wit and an even sharper tongue, she still found a way to use it only when needed.

Hooper has simply just let it fly most of his life without much thought for what his words might do. He's gotten away with it, he knows, because of his perceived status in life.

People want to please. People want something from him. Always, all the time.

His sister is much better at this sort of thing. She'd be great with super real estate agent Grace Jennings, even though his sister owns some of the sharpest tools of them all.

"I'm taking some me time. Spending some time *seeking the counsel of my own company* type of thing. Wanted a big space to do it in style."

A slightly better response.
Not really. Dammit.

"Okay." With a soft clap of her hands, Grace moves on with the tour, crossing in front of Hooper and leaving a storm of secondhand perfume. "As you enter the home, you're greeted by the modest but cozy living room with a real wood fireplace. A great many stories have been told by that fire. Wait." The jacket of her yellow business suit twirls as she spins facing him, snapping her fingers as if the most amazing thought occurred to her. "You're a writer. A great one from what I hear. That all makes perfect sense now. Oh my lord the stories you could tell by that fire. But—"

"Thank you. Very kind words, but I wouldn't say great writer. So-so on a good day. And..." Hooper's smile is forged in discomfort. "I'd be telling those stories to myself. You know, because I'll be alone in such a big house."

"Right, well—"

"It's more than fine. Don't care much for people anyway." Smirks at his half-joke. He doesn't hate all people, only a lot of them.

"Oh." Grace releases an uneasy giggle.

"Sorry. This house is actually perfect. I am working on a new book so that will be nice to talk it out fireside like some half-assed Abe Lincoln."

"Oh, do you dictate your books? Talk them out into your phone or something?"

"No."

"Oh. Okay." Grace picks up the pace of her sales pitch. "Not too cold outside yet, but it will get colder soon. So if you need more firewood, there is plenty in the back of the property if you are willing to go for a quick hike, or you can just call Ronald. Or Ronnie as we call him. His number is hanging in the pantry and on the fireplace. He doesn't live too far away. He's also who to call with any maintenance issues."

Hooper gives a thumbs-up.

Over the years, he's perfected being in a room while being somewhere else at the same time. It's hard on the other people in his life but it works for him. He's comfortable being a million miles away thinking of a book he's working on or whatever story might be percolating while other people are trying to connect with him.

This art of mentally removing himself from a room has ended a few relationships over the years. Marriages fall under the umbrella category of relationships, to be clear. Today's mental drifting is different, however. He knows the distance he's created from this room isn't about his book. Not completely.

Grace goes on to tell him about the dining room near the door to the garage and the table made of reclaimed wood, custom designed to seat twelve rather comfortably. Polished bench seating with the same wood design.

"Truly beautiful," Grace tells him.

Think about how you want to spend your time, the doctor told him.

"Also on the first floor, we have the great room down the hall. Some call it a game room, but I like great room. Large wall-mounted TV, a smaller fireplace, pool table, and a foosball table. Also a bar stocked with what you asked. Hopefully not premature, still need a signature on the rental agreement—nudge, nudge—good bourbon, though. Nice bottles of wine I saw in there too." Grace taps her hand along the granite countertop of the open, sprawling, pristine kitchen. "Of course, you can always do nothing at all. Relaxing is big around here—"

Doing his best to soak in every word, Hooper remains fixed on the view from the living room. High, arching windows rise to meet at a point at the top of the floor-to-ceiling glass. A tall triangle with the panes linked together with polished wood overlooking the mountains. Tall trees in thick rows look as if they are guarding the mountains from any form of attack.

Allison will like it here too.

She won't admit it. Of course not, and there's no way his sister will stay here, not that he'd ask her to, but he does want her to like the place. To feel comfortable with what he's decided to do. At the very least try to understand.

The doctor told him *everyone handles this differently*.

The good doctor also said there are a lot of ways to do this, but finding a plan that works for the patient is what's important. Also mentioned something about that plan being within reason, but Hooper tagged that part as a suggestion rather than strict medical instruction. Regardless, superstar Poconos real estate agent Grace Jennings is right about one thing—*this is truly beautiful*.

"What do you think?" she asks, spreading her arms out wide with a perfectly practiced smile.

"You said there's a bar down the hall?"

"I did."

"Foosball?"

"Yes."

"All that and there's a Ronnie too."

"Only a phone call away."

"No texting?"

"He doesn't like texting."

"Think I like Ronnie."

"He's a lovely man." Grace holds a pen out, stabbing the rental agreement with a bright neon-green nail. "You still sure about the longer rental? We can still change the timeframe—"

"Grace Jennings." Hooper takes the pen. "You could have stopped at *secluded*."

THREE

FRAKES PULLS open the door to the shed.

The boy and girl shield their eyes, sun blasting in like a giant spotlight.

"Morning." Frakes's voice is flat. Dips his head down, hiding as much as he can behind the door. "Mama's got some breakfast for you in the house."

The girl takes the boy's hand. They stand, their thin legs struggling to hold up their tiny frames. They should be shaking, but they won't show an ounce of fear to his man even though they're terrified out of their minds. The girl looks Frakes over. His now-familiar thick blue gloves cover both hands this morning. At least they're clean this time.

She heard him *working* last night.

Her little brother slept beside her while she held him tight, but she heard all the sounds. Labored sounds of Frakes dragging something heavy. Sounds of chopping. Plastic rustling. More chopping, then hacking. She could see the glow of red lights under the shed's door. The smell of exhaust from that old car.

The girl and the boy both know the smells of that car. That stink will forever be part of their memories. The glow of those red lights from inside the trunk will decorate their dreams. They spent hours in that trunk on that horrible night. They held each other, crying and shaking, feeling every jarring bump in the road. All before they were brought here.

"Come on now." Frakes thumbs back toward the house, keeping his eyes down.

Mama once again sits at the beat-up table in the filthy kitchen. Smoking like a chimney. This was the last thing they saw last night. One of the first things they've seen today. It's like nothing has changed. Only difference now is the light of the day makes it slightly less scary than the endless dark of last night.

The boy squeezes her hand. The girl squeezes back harder.

They both step slow and easy outside of the of shed. The light hurts a little worse out here as their eyes adjust. The boy doesn't talk, at least he hasn't since that night. She gets it. She doesn't know if he hates the shed as much as she does, but she guesses he does.

How could he like it in there?

All those sounds from outside. The horrible smells that fill their nostrils. The crushing feeling of not knowing when that rusty metal door is going to open again.

"Get you some eggs and shit off the stove," Mama calls out, waving her hand torch toward the skillet.

The girl looks up at Frakes.

He's like a giant. A monster from the movies her parents won't let her watch. At least they didn't use to. His face is scary. He gets so mad so easy. She wants to say plenty to this monster man, but she doesn't. She keeps her answers and responses to as few words as possible, if any words are used at all.

The voices of her parents echo in her mind. Even though they aren't here, she pretends they are telling her what to do. Like they are standing right next to her and her brother. She does her best to imagine what they'd say.

The girl gives her younger brother's arm a slight tug, inching him toward the house. He doesn't want to go inside but does what his sister wants. Both take tiny steps, inching closer and closer to the house. Feet more dragging than walking. Hunger overpowering their fears.

"You're going to be fine." Frakes tries to sound like how people talk to kids on television. "I won't let anybody hurt you."

The girl stops.

Her feet plant into the ground.

She's never known absolute rage before. It came on so fast. As if there were a click inside her head. It was dull but louder than anything she's ever heard in her life. Not sure she understands what that click means, but there's a burning in her stomach. Her entire body shakes as the temperature of her skin rises. Even the tips of her ears feel like fire.

She can't find the words. Can't form a single word to say as her body vibrates. Her brother looks to her. His eyes pop wide like he's never seen her like this.

The girl looks back to Frakes.

Frakes locks eyes with her. He nods. She's mad. Understandable. She's got every right to be, but she'll come around. This is her home now.

Better than the alternative. He slips his hand inside his pocket, feeling the phone the girl threw at him last night.

A sound stops him cold.

Frakes whips his head around toward the other side of the house. There's a rumble of a car coming. It's close. Really close. They can hear the tires rolling to a stop.

Nobody comes out here.

Frakes bumps into the girl, almost knocking her down as he moves to get a better look. Mama rushes out, grabs the boy and the girl by the arms and drags them inside like rag dolls. She shuts the door, pulling the blinds closed.

Frakes peels off his gloves, tossing them into a bucket by the shed. He yanks a gun from behind his back. Had it tucked in his least dirty jeans. He grips the gun, keeping it down but ready. Every time he touches a gun, his mind jumps back to basic. Years ago. San Diego. Sunshine. Sand. Shown how to fight by hard men. Great time in his life, until it wasn't. Until the anger pulse got the best of him.

Turning the corner of the house, he raises the gun, tracking the parked vehicle.

Shaking his head in disgust, he exhales as he lowers his weapon.

A silver, police-issue Ford Explorer is parked in what could generously be described as a driveway. More like a row of unkept grass and rocks loosely marked with some cinder blocks past their prime. A uniformed officer steps out from the vehicle with his hands up high as a show of goodwill. A smile spreads across his face. His skinny, wiry frame moves cocky and loose.

"Easy, Frakes," Officer Tipton says. "Put that smoke wagon away."

"What the hell are you—"

"Got an emergency."

"You don't say." Frakes feels his anger pulse.

"I do say."

Officer Tipton waves Frakes over to join him at the back of the Explorer.

INSIDE THE HOUSE, the girl and boy can hear some things but not everything. They've never seen or heard of this Officer Tipton before. The girl's insides bounce and dance.

The police are here.

We're safe.

She nudges her little brother and smiles. The first smile she's had since they were brought here.

We can go home, she thinks.

Then it hits her. They don't have a home to go home to. She looks into her brother's eyes, fighting not to show her crumbling feelings as they break apart and fall.

Mama stands near the kitchen window peeking through the blinds at Frakes and Officer Tipton. For the first time, her attention isn't zeroed in on them. The girl watches, studying Mama. The woman is not concerned with being seen by the officer. She's not even slightly worried that the police are here. But she does look back to the girl and her brother every second or two. Like she wants to make sure they don't go anywhere.

Why?

The girl concentrates on what's going on outside.

"Go on, get something to eat," Mama whisper-barks to them. "But take it to the back room. Shut the door. Stay out of the windows."

The girl doesn't understand. The woman doesn't seem worried about the police being here but doesn't want the police to see them. Why doesn't she want the officer to know about her and her brother?

Mama looks at them hard. She ignites her hand torch, creeping it closer to their faces. "Do as I say." Mama sneers. "I'll put some fire to you."

The girl pulls her brother back, nodding her head. She picks up a plate and hands it to her brother. Sure, he's taller than she is, but he's still her little brother, and she is more than sure that woman would light them both on fire without thinking twice about it.

Outside, they hear Frakes and Tipton talk, then stop, then there's what sounds like them struggling with something in the car. Mama looks to the window, then back down at the girl and boy.

"You know what..." Mama snatches the plates away. "Just get."

The girl's and boy's expressions melt. They're hungry.

Mama shakes her head no, then shoves them both toward the back. "Go, dammit."

FRAKES AND TIPTON wrestle a man out of the back of the Explorer.

Still a lot of fight in the guy. Gagged, hands bound, bleeding and bruised. Sweat pours down the man's face. His dirty T-shirt is drenched. The man is big—not Frakes big, but big—and is quite a handful to get out from the back of Tipton's SUV. They dump him next to the rear bumper. The man's teeth bite down on the gag. Screams held in check. His eyes burn hate.

Frakes looks to Tipton.

"Hauk says this guy's the guy. Wants him gone." Tipton gives the man a kick. "All the way gone."

Frakes nods, chewing on the inside of his cheek, trying to hold back saying something he doesn't want said. Something like how he just made a couple of men go *all the way gone*. Just like Hauk said to do with them too. Frakes was up early as hell this morning taking care of it and now Tipton shows up with a new problem to make gone. It's not the work, Frakes doesn't mind the work, it's that there never seems to be an end to it. Can't make everyone who pisses Hauk off go away.

Frakes's eyes gloss over.

He thinks of the night Tipton and Hauk took him to a house. Not that long ago. Thinks of the boy and the girl. Frakes shakes loose the anger pulse thumping back to life.

"You shouldn't come out here like this," Frakes says. "We said you'd call first. Call on that special cell Hauk gave us."

"I know what we said but sometimes things change." Tipton shakes his head. "You need to work on your flexibility. Be like water." Impressed with himself and his big knowledge. "Heard that on some podcast my girl turned me onto. Be like water over stones or whatever. Besides..." Tipton looks over the house, taking in the near-squalor of the place. "You trying to keep this little slice of paradise a secret or something?"

"Don't like visitors. That's all."

"That a fact?"

Frakes nods.

"Well, buddy." Tipton slaps a hand on Frakes's big shoulder. "You don't make the rules around here, or anywhere for that matter. Hauk has that role all filled up."

Frakes stares at Tipton's hand that still rests on his shoulder. Looks like a bug that's landed on a truck.

Anger pulse pounds.

There's a hard fall back down into the deep pit of his thoughts. Calm and dark. Frakes's private perversion of peace. Cold thoughts lead to cold feelings. Icy feelings stroll the length of his spine before tickling the back of his white-hot, anger-pulse mind.

Frakes wants to tear off Tipton's arm and beat him to death with it.

THE GIRL and boy slip away from the kitchen.

They can still hear Frakes and the policeman talking outside. The girl eyes the front door. It's only a few feet away. The doorknob looks huge to her. Like a target waiting for them to strike.

Mama is still in the kitchen.

The girl can hear that scary old woman pacing back and forth. The room that Mama ordered them to go into is to the left. Frakes and Mama have put her and her brother in there to stay sometimes. It's not great. Better than the shed, but not great. The window in that room is covered in aluminum foil and old blankets. No light is allowed in but there's a bed with an old TV with a rabbit ears antenna. Gets two fuzzy channels—three if you use your imagination— they get to watch if they are good. Not that they are any of the channels they like, but again, better than the shed.

The girl knows she and her brother don't have much time. This might be the moment she's been thinking about every night. Hoping for ever since the night they were brought here. Might not get another chance.

Opportunities don't come around all the time, her dad told her one time. *Gotta snatch them up like diamonds.*

"Diamonds," she whispers to herself, eyeballing the doorknob.

Holding up a single finger, she gets her brother's attention, then points down at his feet, letting him know to stay there. The boy nods, confused, but he does what his sister says.

The girl slips over to the room where that woman told them to go. Flipping on the old television, she closes the room's door as she steps back out. Might not work, but it'll at least look like they are in there.

Taking her brother's hand, she directs him to the front door. She feels his body shiver. As she places her hand on the doorknob, she gets down close to her brother's face. She feels her parents next to her. Silent encouragement. Calm, smart words fill her mind. Words she knows they would want her to hear.

"I'm going to open this door."

Her brother shakes his head back and forth. Terrified. She gets it.

"What did Daddy say about opportunities?"

The boy stops shaking his head, remembering. She can almost see the word enter his brain. His shaking head turns to a nod. His face shifts from terror to a crack of a smile.

Diamonds, he silently mouths.

"When I open the door, let's find that policeman. Okay?"

The boy nods again. Trying to be brave or at least look it.

She's scared too but doesn't want him to see it.

Opening the door slow and quiet, she looks back at the kitchen making sure that scary Mama is still there. The boy and girl slip outside, small feet making soft steps. The girl closes the door behind her, making as little noise as possible. Now that they're outside the house, they can really hear Frakes and the policeman.

The boy looks to her for what to do next.

She can see the other side of the house now. The big police SUV is still there but Frakes and the policeman are not.

Where are they?

That familiar dragging sound spins her around.

It's them. Frakes and the policeman are standing over something in the woods to the left of the house. She focuses on the policeman. Her face drops. He's talking with Frakes. Like they're friends or something. He's smiling. Maybe laughing. Has his hand on Frakes's big shoulder.

Frakes stands still like a hulking statue. Not smiling or laughing. There's another man on the ground, kneeling on a plastic square spread out under him. Something tied around his mouth. Hands behind his back. Frakes hands the policeman something. She doesn't know what they're called but it looks like one the biggest knives she's ever seen. They both have one. Long, wide blades with handles wrapped with silver tape of some kind.

The girl's eyes pop wide. She bites back a scream.

She hides her brother's eyes. "Cover your ears," she whispers to him. She wishes she could cover her own as she closes her eyes. Her body shudders.

It's the sounds of it all. A muffled cry mixed with a scream. Sounds like a wounded animal. There's a thick thump. A chop.

She opens one eye. One too many.

Sees the large blades go up and down. One after the other. The biggest knives she's ever seen rise and fall. Big knives held by Frakes and the policeman. The muffled screams stop, but the thumps keep going.

Her blood runs cold.

"Run," her trembling voice says into her brother's ear.

The girl and boy run into the woods with everything they have.

FOUR

"Your positive this is enough house?"

Allison cranes her neck, admiring the height of the ceiling, then turns, checking out the section of the house she can see before landing her gaze back on Hooper. Her hands are planted on the granite kitchen countertop, eyebrows raised, waiting for whatever mountain of crap her brother is about unload.

Hooper pretends she didn't say anything. He's done that a lot over the years, perfected his technique to an all-pro level. Drives her insane. Allison tucks her chestnut brown hair behind her ear, adjusts her glasses, then clucks her tongue, staring at Hooper, forcing a reply from her brother. She can play this game all day.

"You don't like it?" He sips some bourbon

from a crystal glass he found. It's got good weight, much like coffee mugs. The heft and feel are important in Hooper's liquid life.

"No, no. Not that I don't like it. Super fun place, of course, but it's a little much, don't you think?"

Hooper shrugs, passes her the glass. She takes a hit, almost gives it back, then takes another hit. Tightening her grip around the glass, she nods while pressing lips together, acknowledging this is the *good stuff*.

"It's not a damn castle or anything. Kinda cozy, really... when you get used to it." He pushes his chin toward the long hallway. "I'll just go to the bar and get a glass for myself."

"Sorry. The *bar*?"

He waves for her to join him, enjoying all of this a little more than he should.

Allison follows him down the hall into a room that could best be described as a fun house for adults who are children. There's a long, polished oak bar with a wall-sized mirror behind it. Soft lighting. Foosball and a burgundy-felted pool table sit waiting for a game. On the far wall is a 65-inch TV with two large well-positioned brown leather couches with their backs pushed together.

One faces the TV wall, the other faces the bar.

"Unbelievable," she mutters, taking another sip. "Do I want to know how much?"

"You do not."

"You tell the doctor you were here?"

"I did not."

Allison tries to find some eye contact, but Hooper isn't giving up any freely. A true master at avoidance, she knows. Instead, he presses a button on the bar. The massive curtains pull apart, revealing yet another jaw-dropping view. His sister won't let him see how impressed she is. Won't give him and his show an ounce of awe no matter how badly he wants a reaction.

"You going to have that conversation?" She presses the point, eyes locked on the mountains and thick trees outside the window. "With the doctor. Your doctor, to be clear."

Allison has been running the business side of Hooper's publishing life for a few years now. Left a pretty cushy gig at a consulting firm in Chicago to join him in New York. She studied law but had really taken a shine to the media side of the firm where she worked.

Her brother's books were really taking off when he called her. Hollywood wanted to start making deals, international publishing rights in every country on the planet were calling, global book tours, talk shows, too many podcast requests to keep track of, and of course, the umbrella subject of branding and so on.

Hooper never had much of a mind for the dollars-and-cents side of life. Allison always did. While she marvels at her creative-as-hell brother, he has always been taken back by the sister who's smarter than the smartest person in any room he's ever been in.

Pretty much been that way their whole lives.

Hooper is only a year or so older so it's not like he's the classic older brother, but she's had to develop a quick wit to keep up with him. More out of household survival than anything else. If Hooper was being honest, she's blown past him more than a few times. He won't concede the war, but she's won many a battle along the way.

"I'm not supposed to see him for another week or so." Hooper pours himself a fresh glass, then motions to add a little to hers. "He's fine. He's a big boy."

"More concerned about you?"

"I'm an aging child. This has been established."

She doesn't argue. Lets him put a little in her glass. They clink crystal.

"How long?"

"One more time?"

"How long are you renting this place?"

"Not really important." Hooper's shoulders inch up.

"Kind of think it is."

"Why?"

"Is it a damn secret?"

"Does it fucking matter?"

Allison takes a half step back. Eyebrows up, head cocked. Hooper looks away.

His booming response hangs in the air. Those four words came out much harder than he thought they would, or should have. An out-of-character bark. Doesn't like the way he sounded or how it felt. The way he talked to her. An ugly taste coats his tongue. He shakes his head, trying to erase the sudden surge of frustration that came on without warning.

Takes a drink. Resets. Raises a finger.

"Can I get the line again?" He smirks. "I can do it better."

Allison smirks a tight nod—a familiar game between them—closes her eyes, grabs a pinch of air between her fingers while pulling her hand down in front of her face. No idea what that actually does, but she's seen actresses do it all the time.

"How long are you renting this place?" Perfect match of her previous tone and expression, as if hitting rewind.

"Fifteen months," he responds, bright and cheery.

Allison nods again, this time setting her glass down without the actress bit.

"Fifteen months, huh? Wow. That's very specific."

"Is it?"

"Incredibly."

"Odd."

"Not a couple of weeks? A month? Not six months or twelve for that matter."

"I'm working on a book. You knew that, right? Pretty sure you knew that."

"I did know that. Also know you've never taken fifteen months to write a book." She pours herself some more, then starts wearing out the overpriced faux bearskin rug. "Sure, you've dicked around for months and months burning your deadlines, then you'll write a four-hundred-page masterpiece in a few weeks. You've also pushed deadlines back a year or more—of course,

I get to smooth it all out with the publisher, pitching the bullshit *delicate genius* story—but you have never, ever taken exactly fifteen months to write a book."

"I feel like you're picking away at something here." Hooper drops himself into the cushy brown leather of the couch, glass raised high, careful to not to spill his drink.

"Really?" Allison drops into the couch next to him, glass held high as well. "You're going to make me say it?"

"If it'll make you feel better."

"The doctor said twelve to fifteen months."

"I'm trying to be optimistic. Like you told me."

They sit, sipping bourbon, letting the silence inflate like a balloon. A faint tick from a clock can be heard from the next room over. Hooper hadn't noticed it until now. He glances toward his sister. Watching her, he knows her mind is relentlessly working this all through. Always on the job, her mind is. Grinding. Spinning. She'll have something to say soon that will level the room.

Allison finally snaps the quiet like a twig.

"Mom would know what to say right now."

Hooper grins. *And there it is.*

"She would," he says, pushing back the

forming tears. "Dad wouldn't, but he'd have a solid one-liner about canned soup or a flowery quote from a sixties folk singer."

"Yeah." Allison snickers. "You think he actually liked folk songs?"

"No. Not at all." Hooper allows a smile.

"That's what was so great about it."

Hooper sips with agreement. Thinks about their dad's last day. How the two of them sat like they are now... in the hospital. He was twelve. She was eleven. Hooper shakes it off, changes direction on the conversation.

"You remember that guy I was friends with in high school?"

"I don't know, you had so many friends."

"I had one. Adam."

"Oh yeah." She smiles. "Yes. I do remember sweet, sweet Adam."

"He always said you were nerd-hot."

"Are you kidding me?" she says, whipping her head around to him. "Now you're telling me this? He was simply hot-hot."

"Still is."

"You're such a gifted asshole."

"Sorry. Adam's words just occurred to me." Hooper grins. "I want to make sure you know these things. You know, before I go."

"Stop talking."

Hooper drinks his bourbon, letting the good burn roll while loving all this in his own sick little twisted way. Allison turns away but still manages to fire off death-stare-daggers at him through the mirror.

The silence returns, giving them the space for their minds to churn. Welcomed or not. Turning thoughts and memories flip, climbing over and on top of one another. Odd blends of happiness and sadness mixed together. Flashes of good and bad.

"What is your plan?" she asks, exhaustion settling into her voice.

"About?"

"Oh my God."

"Oh, you mean about Johnny?"

"Yes. Of course." Allison shakes her head, full exhaustion reached, meltdown on the horizon. "What do you plan to do, in order to avoid dealing with reality, about an imaginary serial killer you've created named Johnny Psycho who's coming to kill you?"

"Thank you for asking, Allison." Hooper smiles, so pleased with himself. "I plan on hiding from him here and writing that book I told you about."

"Writers are so fucking weird."

Hooper thought that imagining a killer coming for him was much more interesting than the truth. Reality is shit. The real-life, garbage plotline of his impending shit-health-induced demise is so boring. So cliché. Been done so many times by much better writers, in his opinion.

They stare at one another through the massive mirror behind the bar.

Brother and sister.

For better or worse. Sickness and in health. Their faces peek at one another between the bottles. The two of them sitting on a couch in a rented mansion in the woods sipping crazy expensive bourbon from even more insanely expensive glasses. Neither fully understanding how they got here.

Hooper holds up a shiny, new gold key pinched between his fingers.

"No." Allison takes a swig. "Don't want or need a key to this big, stupid house."

"Just take it. Please."

Allison studies the key, then Hooper's half-assed attempt at a charming smile. She snatches it away from him. They go back to the silence.

Hooper debates dropping some deep quote about how funny life can be but decides to leave it. Maybe he should say something about how much he appreciates everything she's done—all she's done in the past and all she will do in the future. Knowing Allison, anything said would make her uncomfortable and might be held against him. She'd like to hear it, she's not immune to kind words, but she'd ultimately tell him to eat shit or suggest he should go and have sex with himself.

Hooper catches her eyes in the mirror, grins big, then extends a middle finger.

Allison returns the gesture.

Finger up, coupled with 35% of a smile.

FIVE

THE GIRL and boy run with all they have.

Legs pump like tiny pistons, powering them through the thick woods. Racing away from the terrible. Running headlong into what they hope is some form of safety. Some semblance of freedom.

Branches whip and tear at them, while the cool fresh air feels nice as it pushes across their faces. The sun peeks through the tops of the towering trees, warming their cheeks every so often as they pass through the pockets of light. A small pop of heat letting them know the sun still shines on some parts of the world.

They have no idea where they are going or when they will get there.

There is no plan. There's only the one word she told her little brother.

Run.

They haven't stopped since they left the front yard of that awful house and the awful people in it. Only slowing down for a moment here and there. More like going from running to fast walking, but never completely stopping.

The trick is to keeping moving forward, their mom told them once, *even when you fall. Fall forward.*

"Fall forward," the girl whispers to herself.

She turns to her brother. His face hits a new shade of red every time she looks over at him. She imagines her face is doing the same. Pushing herself harder, she moves out in front of him, knowing his sibling need to beat her will drag him along with her. It works. She hears the grunt behind her as he finds a new gear and pulls ahead of her. Not by much, but enough.

His legs are longer but there's no way she's letting her younger brother beat her. Not to mention, deep down inside she knows she has to keep them going. It's on her to keep both of them moving as fast as they can. She pulls ahead by a nose.

The sun is starting to set. They have no idea what time it is.

She remembers floating down a river with her parents a few years ago. They had a cabin. Nothing fancy, but it was nice enough for them. They rented a raft. It was fun until it got a hole in it, started losing air in the middle of the water. Not life-threatening or anything, but it scared her. Her brother was too young to know what was happening, not like now.

He pulls ahead by a hair.

Their mom and dad picked them up out of the water as calm as could be. She thought for sure they were going to drown or never get to dry, safe land or any number of other horrible things she imagined might happen to them. But her mother took her by the hand, showing her she could stand up in the water. It almost came up to her shoulders, but she could touch the bottom with her toes.

Her dad picked up the raft and they ended up walking for miles through the woods back to the man they rented the raft from. Mom held her hand and carried her brother in the other arm. She tried to be brave but her parents saw she was scared. Her dad squeezed her shoulders tight and told her they would find a road or something soon. Just keep moving forward. One foot in front of the other. One. Two. One. Two. One...

Her lips move as she counts. *One. Two. One. Two. One...*

Her legs feel like fire. Her sides hurt.

"We'll find a road or something soon," she tells her brother.

He nods, wiping snot away from under his nose.

They dodge trees, duck branches, avoid the loose rocks the best they can. Gaining more and more skill at running through this terrain with each passing second. She can only imagine what is happening back at that horrible house.

What the large man and his mean mama are doing.

What they are saying right now. He's probably angry. Her too.

She hopes they didn't notice they were gone for a while. At least long enough to give them a good head start. She looks back to see if they're behind them. Nothing back there. She pumps her fist. *One. Two. One. Two. One...*

The girl stumbles and skids to stop, grabbing a tree. Her eyes pop wide.

She fires her free arm out, grabbing her brother's collar and yanking him to a jolting stop.

Up ahead is a house. A really big one. There is a huge window that looks like a triangle in the front. Looks like a superhero's lair dropped in the middle of the woods. A door opens up toward the back side of the house. The girl pulls her brother down next to her. They get low, lying under the cover of the trees.

A woman walks out of the house, runs her hands through her brown hair, then gets in a nice car. She's pretty, with smart-looking glasses, but looks mad about something. The car is silver. Fancy. The girl and boy stand up, sucking in huge gulps of air as the car drives away. *A little fast*, the girl thinks. Oh yeah, that woman is mad.

Their thumping hearts start easing down beat by beat. The boy puts his hands behind his head, stretching his elbows out. The girl does the same. Their dad showed them this little trick.

The fastest way to get the lungs back to good, he said, showing them how.

Dad used to go for a jog before work. He took them a couple of times. She could never understand the difference between jogging and running. It was all hard.

She scans the big house as the fancy, silver car disappears down a road that leads into the woods. She studies every inch of the place. Not sure she's ever seen a house so humongous.

Cupping her hand, she whispers into her brother's ear. "You see anybody?"

He squints. Makes his hands into circles like tiny binoculars. Shakes his head no.

There's another car in the driveway. Black. Looks pretty fancy too. Slick and shiny under what's left of the sun's light. Someone else must be in there. That lady looked nice. Maybe. Mad, but nice. Maybe she was mad at who's in that house. Is the person in that house nice?

She chews the inside of her mouth, thinking it through.

It'll be dark soon. Maybe in an hour or two. There are two large trees next to what she'd call a hill. She's sure there's a better nature name for it, but it looks safe. Or whatever passes for safe right now. At least it'll keep someone from creeping up behind them.

She points the spot out to her brother. He shuffles his feet, rubs his nose on his sleeve, then slumps down next to the bigger tree of the two. He's so tired. She can see it all over his face. She is too, but she knows she can't show it. Her feet ache. Legs throb. It'll get cold soon too. It was cold in the shed at night, but they had a thin blanket to share and the rusty metal walls kept some of the wind out. They don't have any of that here.

There's a big stick on the ground in front of her. She sees another one. Picking one up in each hand, she sits next to her brother, handing him the bigger of the two. *Protection*, she thinks. Even she knows that's not completely true. Better than nothing, but only just north of nothing.

The girl turns around again, looking behind them, peeking up over the hill, wanting to see if the horrible people are behind them. Can't help but wonder if she'll always be looking for them. Always looking behind her. Wondering when that large man and his mama will find them.

They will come looking.

Zero doubt in her mind.

Reliving what she saw at the house before they ran away, a cold shiver rockets up her spine. This is first chance she's had time to even think about it. What that mean man and the policeman were doing to that other poor man. She tries not to think about it all. Tries to force the images out. Squeezes her eyes tight, working hard to push all that ugliness away from her mind the best she can. But she can't do it. Some things stay with you no matter how hard you try. Some memories are written in ink.

The sounds. The thick thumps. The begging.

All hovering in her ears like a bug that won't go away. She knows now that all those sounds she and her brother heard while they were in that shed were probably from the same things. Horrible things going on just outside that shed. Done by that man. All of it only a few feet from where they were sleeping. His *work* they heard him call it. Work done by the man who took their parents away from them.

Lights turn on around the front of the house.

Her brother looks to her. She bites her lip with eyes fixed on the glow.

Is the person in that humongous house mean or nice?

SIX

FRAKES AND MAMA tear through the woods that surround their house.

They don't know which way the kids went. Not sure how long they've been gone. They've been searching for what seems like half the day.

That asshole Tipton was at the house for at least an hour or two. Mama didn't even notice the boy and girl were gone until after he left. Frakes grinds his teeth at the thought. The boy and girl could have a good two-hour head start on them. Maybe as long as three. They're fast, but those short legs won't take them too far.

He looks to Mama.

How could she be so careless? All her talk of him being lazy, him being dumb for what he's done. All her bullshit and she does this? He wants to shake her. Scream into her face. She knows damn well what's at stake here. What the cost of losing them will be. What will happen if that boy and girl get free. If they talk.

Mama's eyes dance. Puffing away at her beloved smoke, her head makes quick, jerky turns scanning the thick woods. Needle in a haystack doesn't cover it. Her face balls up in an angry brand of worry. Frakes looks her over. Oh yeah, she's aware of what's on the line here.

She knows she done things wrong, he thinks.

Frakes has been on a hunt like this before. Hunted many adults like this, but this is the first time looking for littles. Big difference is he usually has the benefit of people like Tipton or some of Hauk's other people to help. Calling them now is a last resort sort of thing. Deep down, Frakes knows he might not have a choice.

Think.

Those littles don't know where they are.

They don't know this area at all.

Their eyes were covered in the trunk of the car on the way to the house. Frakes made sure he took plenty of unnecessary turns and detours—even turned around in a few circles in an open field off the highway—just in case the boy and the girl were paying attention. He knew they were smart little ones, but were they smart enough to decipher all that? Doubtful.

"Are you going to call this in?" Mama coughs. Lungs fighting the years of abuse.

Frakes doesn't answer.

He picks up a broken twig. Sees a rock that's been turned over with fresher ground underneath. They could have gone this way. Or it could be from a passing animal. Or it could have been Mama when they came through here the first time around. Shuffling her damn feet the way she does.

"Are you?" she presses. "We ain't doing much damn good out here. Sun's almost all the way closed for the day."

You did this! He wants to yell it so loud that it blows out the Lord's ears.

He keeps it to himself. Pushes it all down. She's right about calling it in and he knows it. But if there is even the slightest of chances he can find them on his own, he has to try. Hauk doesn't know anything about the boy and girl being held at his house.

Or any of the rest it for that matter.

Hauk is not a forgiving sort of man, nor has anyone ever referred to him as understanding. Frakes has been a loyal soldier for years, but

Hauk will not hesitate to take care of loose ends. No matter if Frakes is the one who usually ties up those loose ends.

"Hey." Mama stops, hands on her knees. "We've been out here wandering around forever. Doing damn circles around the house."

Frakes keeps moving. Adjusts his gun tucked behind his back.

"If you don't call it in, I will. This is bullshit."

Frakes moves up on her in a snap. Stops himself just short of putting his hands on her. As if a leash is holding him back. She takes a stumbling step backward, surprised by her son's speed and aggression. His spine is straight, eyes wild, showing her the pitch-black of her son's eyes.

"What?" Her voice cracks.

"I will find them."

"Will you now?"

Frakes nods. The anger pulse vibrates throughout his entire body.

"Do not call it in."

"Or what?" she asks, lighting up a smoke with her hand torch. "What if I do?"

"I'm asking you nice."

"Feels a little like you're warning me, boy."

"No." Frakes takes a step back, fighting like

hell to reel himself in. "No, Mama. I'm not. I'm asking you. We're in this thing together. Right?"

Mama looks away.

"Right?"

Mama blows out a long trail of smoke. Finally gives a nod in agreement.

"Now. I'm going to find those kids, Mama."

"And if you don't?"

"Then we are dead."

Mama considers her son's words with a glaze coating her stare out into a void only she can see. Looking through Frakes. Past this world and her son as if he's blending into the setting sun.

"Not me, boy. You did what you did."

SEVEN

Hooper presses his forehead against the floor-to-ceiling living room window.

He imagines falling through.

Him landing on top of the shattered glass. Or maybe he'd fall faster and the glass would land on him and shatter. Of course, at some point, the large pane of glass would have to turn or flip, allowing him to pass. Interesting to think about.

He'd rather none of that actually happen, but it's a fun scene to let his puppy of a mind play with. He also enjoys the cool glass on his forehead. Recently, every so often, he's noticed his temperature will spike and his head will spin just a bit, making him seek the stability of something, well, stable. Which is how he got to thinking about the glass giving way to his tumbling demise.

The lights that run along the house give the land a really cool effect. A manmade glow strapped to the sides of this mansion dropped deep into the middle of so much natural beauty. He has no idea how the lights turned on, or why, or how to turn them off. Would have been nice if the super agent had mentioned it. Maybe she did. Hooper tuned out about halfway through. But the lights are a nice touch.

Taking a seat in the ultra-cushy, red wine-colored chair by the window, Hooper enjoys his new beverage choice. Switching to coffee was the answer. The bourbon, no matter how good it was, had started to get him a little fuzzy.

The medication already offered fuzz and buzz to his thinking. Coupled with the occasional flare of nausea, along with spins and temperature jump as previously noted. He has also noticed he gets tired more easily. As he sips his coffee—he found the machine on the counter; not as good as that place in town, but not terrible —he thinks of the last run he took in New York. A nice cool morning run through the park. His mind drifts.

Allison will come around.

He's dumped a lot on her. No doubt. She needs to process, give it all a good think. Then she'll come around to understanding his thinking on this.

Hopefully.

Not like he's given her any solid options, really. He knows he should have discussed his plans with her. At the very least told her something about what he was thinking of doing before he did it. Not only are they brother and sister, they are business partners of sorts. Thoughtfulness is something he's struggled with through the years.

A former wife told him once that his brief moments of caring were great, but consistency goes a long way. He didn't understand what she meant. They were young. Got hitched when he was in his late twenties, she just out of college at twenty-two. He taught a class and she was a student in crazy-stupid awe of him. The cliché of it all bothered the hell out of him. Then, after having coffee a few times, a dinner or two, he grew to understand why clichés become clichés.

He'd written a novel, his first, that had done okay, good sales. Not enough to get him out of the day gig of teaching at a state school, but it was well received. She was smart, and yes, beautiful, and she loved him. And Hooper screwed it all up. They separated just shy of fourteen months.

That bonfire of a relationship was the first of several.

Hooper pushes himself up from the cushy chair. Glad no one was around to see how much he struggled to get up. Made an old man noise as he did it, too, then topped it off by rubbing his lower back. Grunting at himself.

"Pull it together, Hooper."

He did a garbage job of packing before coming here. He can hear Allison saying those exact words in his head, and she's right of course. There's a backpack stuffed with things that don't belong together. There's a pair of shoes with a toothbrush inside them. A Nike bag stuffed with odds and ends. A bunch of shirts on hangers that he laid down in the backseat of the car and three canvas grocery sacks with everything from random toiletries to a few pairs of jeans. He only hopes that underwear is somewhere inside that hurricane.

One of the grocery sacks carries his much-hated medications.

All the meds that will help ward off Johnny Psycho.

"Thirty-two pills a day keep Johnny away."

He digs through the rattling bottles of pills, setting them out one by one. The doctors and nurses gave him all the instructions. He took it all in, soaking in every word. He did much better than when the super real estate agent was telling him things.

Allison was there at the doctor's office too, which helped a lot. Between the two of them, they cracked the code on the scheduling of the meds. Meaning Allison did the majority of the cracking. She put together a tight, color-coded spreadsheet and printed it out for him to have knowing he'd never pull it up on a laptop or tablet. He thanked her, and then of course left it at home. He'll ask her for another copy after she has that big *come around* moment he's convinced she will have soon.

He snaps his fingers. Mutters a dammit to himself. He forgot that his collection of sneakers is in the trunk of his car. There're ten pairs. Maybe it's a collection, maybe it's not, depends on the person, he supposes, but he loves his sneakers. His standard uniform is jeans, a button-down shirt and a selection from the collection chosen based on his mood or what he's writing for the day. Explaining which pair goes with what writing is impossible; it's just something he knows.

Setting his coffee down, he grabs his keys.

The night air is crisp. Breathing in deeply, he can't help being amazed by how unique and wonderful the smells are around here. So much better than the city. Understatement of the century. In a much different way, the quiet gets to him too. He's never experienced booming silence like being out here. So quiet it hums. The phrase *middle of nowhere* is overused, but it works here.

Holding down the button, the trunk pops open. Inside are a row of his beloved sneakers. He's amazed at how well they stayed in line during the trip. There's also another grocery sack with some odds and ends, but his eyes zero in on something. Quickly, he realizes there's something else he forgot in his trunk.

"Hey there," a perky, yet low voice says.

Hooper turns, almost falling. The meds cause his balance to be off at times too.

"Easy. Sorry. I'm Ronald," the man says, holding out a big, rough hand. "But Ronnie is better."

The super real estate agent mentioned him. His own personal Ronnie. Hooper holds his heart like a character in a Tennessee Williams play who got such a fright.

"Didn't mean to scare you, buddy."

"No, no." Hooper finds some air for his lungs. Shakes Ronnie's hand. "No, I'm good. I was told you were around."

"Oh yeah, I'm around, all right. Meant to come earlier. Introduce myself and all that." Ronnie's smile is big and genuine. Looks right out central casting. Fifty pushing sixty with broad shoulders, mostly gray beard, and build like a brick shithouse. "The real estate agent probably told you, but I take care of maintenance and whatnot. Always working. Rarely sleeping."

"She mentioned it, yeah."

"Everything good with the house?"

"I think so."

"Good."

"Yeah, it is good."

Hooper knows this is when someone better at this would say something nice or funny, or hell, say anything. But the two men silently nod and smile awkwardly at one another.

"Hear you're a writer."

"I am."

"I read a lot. Non-fiction mostly. Military."

"Nice."

More nodding.

"Okay." Ronnie claps his hands. "That's all I've got. She tell you about the firewood?"

"She did but—"

"There's a pile on the other side of the house I started chopping the other day. Left my gear in the storage room. The door is by the alarm panel, if you feel like cutting some yourself. Some folks think it's great exercise to get out there and hack away."

"You mean Manhattan hipster douchebags who want to be outdoorsmen for thirty minutes, then go back to streaming whatever on Wi-Fi."

"Yeah, those."

They both smile big, a connection cutting through the social awkwardness. Hooper can tell there's a whole lot of worldliness in Ronnie's eyes. Nice guy but he's seen things. There's a lot of stories a guy like Hooper can build from talking to a guy like him. That, and there's an honesty to him that Hooper misses from the good people of Manhattan. He used to know people like Ronnie growing up. Good people.

His mind flashes to a memory. One of his dad telling him and Allison mildly crude jokes on the way to the movies. He was maybe eight or so.

"You want a drink?" Hooper asks, pushing

his head back toward the house. The question left his mouth before he even knew he asked it. Very unlike him.

"I know you've got some good hooch in there, so thank you, but I've got to get to the other properties." Ronnie shakes Hooper's hand. "I don't drink, but I'll take a rain check on some tea if you can spare it."

"Anytime, Ronnie."

As Ronnie leaves, slipping into the night, Hooper turns his attention back to the trunk of his car. His mind slips back to where he was. As his shoulders slump, he can feel his mood change as if a button was pushed.

There's a silk pillowcase, lumpy from what's inside.

Hooper's fingers run over the silk, feeling the contents. Picking up the case, he holds it open, rocking it back and forth ever so slightly. His eyes glaze, putting him in a trance-like state as he stares inside the pillowcase.

A black .357 slips and slides in the silk.

A single golden bullet rolls alongside the gun. The lone bullet he was saving for if, or when, Johnny Psycho comes calling.

Hooper invented the story about how deranged Johnny, an unstoppable killing machine, escaped a mental institution to hunt him down after reading one of his books. A real '80s slasher type of thing, not even a good one, but this flimsy backstory helps Hooper process. Even went as far as inventing a voice. In his head, Johnny sounds like the perfect mix of every cinematic psychopath that used to scare the hell out of him during childhood. Playful hiss and all.

Silly, silly Hooper.

Will make such a pretty, pretty corpse.

Easier for Hooper to get his head around the idea of a deranged killer chasing him than the numbing truth. No matter how insane that might sound to others.

It comforts him to have the gun, if he's being honest, but he doesn't know if he'd ever do it. Never thought of himself as an *easy way out* sort of guy. Of course, up until recently he's never sat on a cold, hard doctor's table and been told cold, hard things before.

Hardest words a person will ever hear. Never heard words like *terminal* or *diagnosed* wrapped in tones of clinical warmth. Pamphlets were given. Prescriptions sent in. Follow-up visits. Support groups suggested.

How long? Hooper asked.

Ten to fifteen months, hopefully longer but

maybe less. Twenty-two thousand Americans are diagnosed each year. Fifteen thousand die within twelve months. The lucky ones, about one in ten, live longer. There are some procedures that have had some success—

How bad?

What? the doctor asked.

How fucking bad will it get? Hooper yelled. He never yells.

Hooper saw a flash in the doctor's eyes before he even uttered another word. The good doctor ready to roll into a speech he'd given many times, possibly that day. Was probably about to give Hooper a verbal tour much like super special agent Grace Jennings. Hooper had stopped him before he started. Spared himself another dive-bomb of stats and practiced, clumsily paced empathy.

Bad was the answer to how bad things will get. Johnny Psycho bad.

That's all Hooper needed to understand.

Snapping out of it, he folds the pillowcase closed and shoves it in the canvas bag. Does the same with a few pairs of sneakers and gathers the rest in his arms.

He feels a twist in his stomach. Like a fist balling up for a fight. His hands shake as he rushes into the house, shoving everything onto a long dining room table. The room closest to the garage. He whips his arm around and slams the door closed, then spins, falling and catching himself on the side of the table.

Both palms are planted flat on the table while he breathes hard in and out. Every part of him feels like cheesecake—firm, but soft enough to poke a finger through. Thoughts blur and whirl. A relentless stream of everything. No order. No logical progression. Memories and ideas pop like popcorn bouncing off the inside of his skull.

His parents. His first book deal. Allison graduating college.

Signing divorce papers. Friends he's stopped talking to.

The dog he had as a child. Air guitar to Zeppelin in his room. His third wedding in Mexico.

The idea of that story he's wanted to write ever since he was a kid. A story based on something his mom gave him on her deathbed.

Hooper presses his fingers hard on the wood of the table as if trying to dig in. He breathes in deeply through his nose, then slow out through his mouth. Fighting the pounding of his heart.

There are pills for this on the counter. If he can get there. He squeezes his eyes closed.

The doctors.

Timeframes of what's left of his life.

The cop friend who gave him that gun as a gift. An old school .357, he said. Hooper packing it and bringing only one bullet.

There's a soft knock.

Hooper spins toward the front door, almost falling to the floor once again. Jolted away from the mudslide of thoughts by this unexpected knock at the door. Nobody knows he's here except for Allison. No way she'd come back. Not tonight. A bead of sweat rolls down his back.

Is it Ronnie? Changed his mind on that tea?

The super real estate agent told him about the security cameras, but he wasn't really listening. Maybe there's a screen in the kitchen. He can't remember. Not sure his cheesecake legs will get him there.

Another soft knock.

Hooper pulls himself together the best he can. Gives his face a tiny slap from cheek to cheek and works to steady himself, holding his hands out to his sides. Uses the walls for balance to walk himself to the door like he's in a small-town carnival funhouse. Hooper presses an eye to the peephole.

Can only see the top of one head. Can barely see the hair of another.

What the hell?

Hooper opens the door.

A girl and a boy stand on the porch staring up at him.

EIGHT

THE GIRL and boy look up at Hooper.

Two small, blank-faced statues void of any readable expression. Staring, waiting for him to do or say something. As if looking for a grown-up to know what do to.

For a moment, Hooper thinks they might be selling something. Candy bars for some shitty band trip or whatever. Magazine subscriptions, if that's even a thing anymore. It's been a long day and he'd rather not deal with whatever this is. Hooper starts to speak and then stops himself, thinking what he had teed up was not cool for when speaking with children.

Hooper feels something is off here. There's something different with these kids. They're looking for something, but it's not money for a school thing.

Something is not okay.

The boy's eyes flutter, his body shakes, only a little bit, then stops. Like he realized he was doing it and stopped himself. The girl holds the boy's hand, fingers locking with his. The boy squeezes. She squeezes back tighter. The girl never looked his way, no words uttered between them. It's as if she knew he needed it.

Hooper's thick layers of surface cynicism fade. No question something else is going on here with these kids. Hooper takes a beat, takes a step back, his writer mind taking in all the details of them under the light of the porch.

They look so tired.

Too tired for how young they are.

Dirt is clumped and clinging to their tiny faces. There's an anxious emptiness to their eyes. A look of lost, perhaps. Hidden desperation, maybe. Their clothes are a mess. Looks like they've slept in them for days, if not longer. The girl's golden-brown hair is decorated by darker, browner leaves, while the boy's hair is mostly matted down, unruly as hell in other spots. Their dirty faces have streaks of shine where sweat has broken through the earthy cake.

Hooper has never been good with guessing kids' ages—or good with kids period—but he thinks they are maybe eight or so.

"Hi," Hooper finally says. Sounds more like a question than a greeting.

The boy turns to his sister, then back at him. The girl smiles. Forced, nothing honest about it, but she's trying. She elbows the boy. He flashes a quick, truly awful smile. Like he ate something horrible his mom made but knew he needed to shine on how wonderful it was.

Neither one says a word.

Hooper pokes his head out from the door, looking to see if there's a car or an adult with them. Finds nothing but nature and that cool glow the lights outside the house provide. The wind whistles through the trees. He brings his eyes back to the children.

"Hi," Hooper says again. No idea what to do with this.

Fairly sure he'd like to return to his nervous breakdown at the dining room table rather than this uncomfortable conversation with the strange children of the woods.

The girl smiles again, this time a little more relaxed, then waves to him. She nudges the boy once more. He cracks another labored but better smile, with a wave to Hooper as well.

"Okay." Hooper grins, offering his own half-hearted wave. "Are you lost?"

There's a sound behind them.

The girl whips around. Almost spins all the way to the ground. Nothing casual about it. Animalistic even.

As if she thought something deadly was behind her. Her expression is no longer blank. She's scared. The boy is too. Hooper steps out from the house, closing the door behind him. He walks to the front of the house, taking a better look around. Scans, looking into the dark for anything that might give him some answers here.

Nothing.

Only the cool breeze blowing around the wonders of nature that seem like they want to swallow the house. There's a rustle of leaves. Clouds breaking apart for the moon to peek through. Some clicks and clacks from various unidentified bugs out there but nothing truly threatening.

Turning back to the girl—she seems to be the one running the show—he moves a little closer. She takes a step back. Careful not to get too close,

Hooper crouches down so he's eye level with her. The boy moves in close to her. Fists gripped tight. She holds out a hand, letting him know it's okay.

"What's your name?"

She doesn't answer. Tears swell as she stares back at Hooper, never breaking eye contact. The boy locks in on him, not liking how close he is to her, or to him for that matter.

Hooper shifts back a bit. They must be brother and sister. They have similar faces. Noses are a match. There's also a look in the boy's eye. Protective uneasiness. Irrational bravery. She's got it too, but she's hiding it better. They are too young to have that strong of a friendship or any tougher-than-nails puppy love interest. Maybe. What the hell does Hooper know?

"Can you talk?"

The girl nods. The boy looks down at his feet.

"Okay." Hooper smiles, nods, trying to show he's not a bad guy. "Can you talk to me?"

The girl nods, looking around again as if searching for threats. Hooper raises his eyebrows, waiting. Seconds tick. The silence drags for what feels like hours.

The girl starts to speak, the word gets caught in her throat, then she tries again.

"Help."

NINE

NINE

THE GIRL and boy take one step inside the house, both keeping their weight on the foot they keep outside on the porch.

Hooper waits, standing a safe distance to the side of them. The children look both ways like crossing a busy highway. Eyes darting, shoulders up, fight or flight. The girl nods to the boy and they place both feet inside the house, taking a small step forward.

Hooper shuts the door behind them.

The kids jump, putting another couple of feet between them and this man they don't know. Hooper puts his hands up on instinct. A show that everything is okay.

The girl takes the boy's hand. They turn, standing in the foyer, their necks straining while trying to take in the enormity of the house. Hooper realizes this just might be a castle in their eyes. Probably only read about places like this in books or seen them in movies.

Although he realizes he's assuming a whole hell of a lot. Perhaps projecting his own penniless, coupon-clipping-with-Mom childhood. His father's death left him, Allison, and their mom with no-end-in-sight debt from medical bills and brought their household income to zero. The bank accounts went to negative numbers more times than their mother let on. He and Allison were older than these kids but not by much.

Maybe these kids come from wealth, but judging by the wideness of their eyes, their dropped jaws and open mouths while looking over the house, he's assuming this place is quite a sight to them. Hell, it was something to behold when Hooper walked in too. He considers giving a tour similar to the one he got from super agent Grace Jennings, but decides this might not be the right audience.

Moving slow and careful, Hooper tilts and weaves around them avoiding getting too close. Treating the children as if they were playing cards stacked into shapes of tiny people. One wrong move could send them tumbling down.

He rubs his hands. Rubs his face. Scrambling for some idea of what he's supposed to do with this situation he's found himself in. Not a lot in Hooper's past to turn to here.

"Would you like something to drink?" Hooper pulls open the door to the Sub-Zero fridge. A half-empty refrigerated vault containing only a sampling of soft drinks, a couple of bottles of overpriced water, and some locally brewed beers. "Haven't made it to the store—guess I should think about that—but they stocked the place with a few things, I think."

He turns back to them.

They haven't moved an inch. Not completely sure they're even breathing. Two tiny slabs of steel bolted to the floor staring back at him, blinking only as necessary. Hooper grabs two bottles of water, deciding the drying sweat mixed with dirt is a solid sign they could use some hydration. Never claimed to be a genius, but he has his moments.

Offering the water, he holds out the bottles for them to take. They remain still, maintaining their statue gaze. The boy turns to the girl. He wants the water but needs to know she's okay with it. The girl looks Hooper over. He can feel her studying everything about him.

Leaning over, Hooper sets the bottles at the end of the kitchen island. A reasonable spot. Almost exactly halfway between him and the children. When they don't make a move for the water, Hooper takes a few steps back, creating an even safer distance between them.

The girl inches a little closer to the bottles, still not sure, eyes never leaving him. Hooper can think of a million different stories explaining what has happened to these children—it's what he does for a living—but as far as what to do with them, he's beyond lost. Of course, right now all he wants is for them to have some damn water and not pass out on this rented floor.

An idea slaps him.

Holding up a finger asking for a second, Hooper opens the fridge and grabs a water identical to the bottles on the counter. He cracks the lid, drinks, then releases an *Ahhhhh* in satisfaction. Not too over the top, but maybe enough to sell the idea. At least hoping this action will show he's not trying to poison or drug the untrusting youth.

That's not a bad book idea, however.

A house in the woods with a crazy dude who poisons children—maybe a take on a dark fairy-tale type of thing. Hooper fights the urge to make a note in his phone. The initial surge of an idea taking flight, he stops just shy of picking up his phone. Not the best time, he realizes, but it's killing him. What would be best is if these woodland children would drink the damn...

It worked.

The girl nods to the boy, snatching both bottles from the kitchen island and handing one to her brother. Hooper can't help but feel a tiny bit of pride. His third wife said she'd never have children with him. He wasn't "properly wired for parenting" she'd tell him after her third nightly white wine. She was British, whip-smart, gorgeous, and colder than cold. Hooper will take this water bottle moment as proof she was wrong, no matter how right he knows she was.

"Now that we're all friendly..." Hooper takes another drink, watching the boy and girl gulp theirs down. "Can we chat about some things?"

"Help," the girl says, as if he'd asked about the weather.

"Okay." Hooper nods, still keeping his distance. "Got that part, but I need more."

The girl falls back into her stare.

She's got a good one, Hooper thinks. It's a hard stare with just a hint of softness. Not angry but not a whole lot of happy in there either. It's a thinking stare from someone who doesn't trust you at all but is willing to hear you out. A look that gives you nothing, telling you that you'll have to work harder to pry anything loose.

"How about names? That's how people get to know people, right?"

The boy wipes his mouth. The girl blinks.

"Can you tell me what I should call you?"

Nothing.

"Is it a secret?"

The boy looks to the girl. Her eyes slip to her brother briefly, then back to Hooper. She shakes her head no. The boy nods, as if that was his answer too.

"Okay." Hooper steps back from the kitchen island. The children take a step back as well. Hooper puts his hands out in front of him. Palms open as if trying to calm frightened animals. "Okay. So, the names aren't a secret. You just don't want to tell me? That the thing?"

The girl nods. The boy follows suit.

"That's fair." Drinks his water. Wants his bourbon.

He isn't getting any closer to figuring out what to do here. His stumbling mind rambles, fumbles for something to even start with. A damn direction would help.

Stop. Think.

What do I actually know?

These two children showed up at his door at night. Alone. They won't talk. They are filthy and appear to be tired. No sign of parents or adult supervision.

He looks them over, scanning them from head to toe, seeing if he's missed a detail that might help him here. He can't be completely sure, but it doesn't look like they have phones on them. Of course, he's not sure what age kids get phones, maybe at birth for all he knows. Frisking them is not really an option, but it is a consideration.

What else? What else do I know?

About kids in general? Less than jack shit. What he does know about is characters. Characters are driven by what they want. Okay. That's something. The girl has made it clear they want the open-ended, non-committal *help.*

Hooper taps the counter with a nervous drum beat. "When you say *help*, can you open that up a bit?"

The girl scrunches her nose.

"I mean *help* can translate into all kinds of things."

Hooper tests them by making a slow-paced

side-to-side movement along his side of the kitchen island. Watching them, making sure they're okay with his movement. The children don't seem to mind.

"Help could mean a bottle of water—check. It could mean you're out of gas and need a lift. Is your car out of juice?"

They shake their heads.

"Okay. That's two possible areas of help pushed out of the way—only a few million to go. How about addiction? People sometimes need help overcoming addiction. Cocaine? You kids slaves to the powder?"

The girl smirks but pulls it back quickly. The boy shakes his head no, trying to hide his smile but fails.

"Good. It's bad stuff, trust me." Feels a new surge. He's getting somewhere. "Do you need help with marital issues? Lots of people have those. How about you two? Spouse got you down?"

The girl and boy smile, shaking their heads in a hard no.

"Thank God. I'm horrible at marriage."

Hooper opens a cabinet that looks like it might have food in it. Not much. There's a bag of Cheetos. Odd, but okay. This might just do. He

picks up the bag and shakes it for the children to
see. The kids' eyes pop wide.

Yes. Hooper stops just short of pumping his
fist.

He slides the bag across the island toward
them. The girl catches it before it falls to the
floor. So, they're hungry too.

Of course they are, dumbass.

But that can't be it. Yes, food and water are
big in this life, but there has to be more to their
story of help than that.

Food, water, shelter have been achieved.
They've nailed the survival basics, but those
don't explain the big, fat *why* of the situation.
Somehow they got lost in the woods. These kids
are not aliens—Hooper's fairly sure—they have to
have some form of a family somewhere. Perhaps
separated from their parents on a camping thing
or they were playing and drifted too far. Maybe
their family is renting something not far from
here. All believable scenarios, but there's something that doesn't add up.

Hooper watches the children crunch away,
faces and fingers growing more and more orange
by the second.

Why won't they talk?

He can understand the whole stranger

danger, the scared and lost feeling, but why won't they at least tell him their names? It's obvious they can. There are no signs of a disability. Why the refusal to tell him anything for that matter? Tell him to call someone or even ask to borrow the phone?

"Would you like to borrow my phone?"

The girl and boy look up, orange dust coating their fingers and the corners of their mouths.

"Is there someone you can call?"

They glance to one another, then plant their eyes back on Hooper.

"Someone I can call? Like your mom and dad?"

The boy begins to shake.

Tears swell at the edges of the girl's eyes as she presses her lips together tight.

Hooper steps back, watching her jaw clench beneath the skin. A cold chill rockets through him watching their little faces morph from the excitement of food back to the blank looks of lost they had at the door. There's a sudden hardness to their eyes now. Defenses back up. Shields have come back online.

"Okay." Hooper puts his hands back up, showing he's still a good guy. Still on their side. "Don't have to use the phone. Not a requirement for food, water, or a roof over your head. Just asking." He cocks his head. "We cool?"

The boy looks to the girl for a verdict.

The girl thinks, then nods. They go back to destroying the bag of orange-dusted greatness. Hooper exhales. Makes a mental note—something happened with the parents. That much is clear. No words needed on that subject.

His mind goes to work. The guesses as to what's happened pile on top of one another. Abuse? Accident? Abandoned? Their reaction was sudden. Like a cord inside them had been tugged. An immediate physical reaction to a simple question about calling their parents.

Hooper chews at the inside of his cheek. His usually dependable, best-selling creative genius mind has been reduced to a jittery lump of useless. He's so damn in over his head. Then it hits him like a freight train. *How could I be so damn thick?* Of course. He needs to bring in the big guns.

Allison.

Allison will know what to do.

His phone sits on the counter behind him. Looking back to the children crunching away, he knows he can't simply pick up the phone and start chatting with his sister. Who knows how that would play with his new guests. Based on how they reacted to the discussion about the phone earlier, a call with Allison might not go over well at all. Think...

The Cheetos have worked something amazing, but I don't have any other food to barter with.

What do I have to work with here?

He looks to the living room.

Television. The world's babysitter.

"Hey, kids." Hooper claps his hands together. The boy jumps. The girl steps back. "How about you guys grab that bag of baked chemical goodness, I'll get the waters, and we'll watch some pixels bounce and dance?"

The children stare back.

Hooper could punch himself in the face. He tries again.

"TV. Let's go into that room, eat Cheetos, and watch us some TV."

The boy smiles huge. The girl is more guarded, but she's interested. The plastic of the bag crinkles as she grips it tight in her tiny hands. Finally, after much internal debate, she nods.

The boy nods too.

Hooper follows up with a single nod of his own as he slips his phone into his back pocket.

TEN

The children huddle together, sunk deep into the worn brown leather.

Moonlight coming in from the windows that seemingly touch the night sky frame them perfectly. The Cheetos bag rests half in her lap and half in his. The bottles of water sit on a wood table, resting on coasters with bears painted on them.

The massive 4K screen takes up almost the entire wall. Hooper fumbled around with the remote for a while—the girl couldn't take it then helped him—finding a SpongeBob marathon. Hooper got lost watching the opening song for a moment but snapped out of it. After a few minutes, he softly announced that he was going to the bathroom. The children might have heard him, he wasn't sure, but he didn't wait for a conversation that wasn't going to come.

Down the hall, Hooper slipped into the room with the bar—he doesn't know what to call it. Game room, maybe? Pacing back and forth, phone held tight to his ear, he talks to Allison.

"What the hell are you talking about?" Sounds of the road seep through the phone. "I *might*—can't stress *might* enough—come back sometime, but no way in hell I'm turning around."

"I know it's a big ask, but I really need you to come back now."

"Run out of your fancy-bitch bourbon already?"

"No. Something has happened—"

"Do I need to call the doctor?"

Her voice turns on a dime from its normal sparing tone to pure concern. Hooper considers lying to get her there faster but stops himself. Even he has limits.

"No. I'm fine, but I need you to come back to the—"

"Big house gets scary at night, doesn't it?"

"Adorable." Resets. Deep breath. "Look, it would be helpful if you'd listen to—"

"No. No, I'm kinda done listening to you. I'm

halfway to New York, not turning around for whatever bullshit emergency you've decided I need to deal with."

"Allison. You don't understand—"

"Oh, pretty sure I do. I'm enjoying the drive home. Nice wide-open road." Hooper hears her crank up Wolf Alice in the car. "I'm going to sing. Loud."

"Allison." He peeks down the hall. "Please."

"I'll come back when I said I'd be back."

"What? You said you might be back sometime."

"Exactly."

The phone goes quiet, like he's holding a brick of metal and glass.

"Allison," he says, even though he knows he's talking to the room.

He calls back. Straight to voicemail. Tries again. Same result. Considers a text—Hey 2 kids showed up. HELP!!!—but stops his thumbs just short from tapping away. Taking a deep breath, hand hovering above the glass, he sends another message.

Allison. Something has happened. I really need your help.

His pacing slows, as does his hope of rein-forcements coming to his aid. Hooper stops in the middle of the room, tossing his phone the couch.

He doesn't know how to help these children. Closing his eyes, he breathes in and out. Balls his fists and releases them on each exhale. Hopes this half-assed meditation will let the answers flow.

It doesn't.

Think...

The children are scared of something. They are alone. They won't call anyone. Hell, they won't even speak to him. They've obviously been running, perhaps away from something.

"Or someone," he whisper-thinks.

Looks to his phone on the couch. He could call the police. That's what people do in situations like this. That is what he'd have a character in his books do.

This is how Hooper relates to the world and he knows it—how would a smart character react to something?

Helps him remove himself from the actual world and, in turn, gives the reading world what it probably wants from him. He does it in interviews too. Finds it works on podcasts, panel discussions at conferences, and book-signing chitchat. The public gets this version of Hooper that is somewhat real but mostly not. He performs how the character of Nicholas Hooper —worldwide best-selling author with movie and streaming deals—would and should behave. There's wit, some substance, but mostly smiles and one-liner bullshit.

A carefully constructed character pieced together for the masses. This is what he wanted to be when he met with the doctors. He wanted to be the character who handles bad news the right way. That guy in the thing who lets the worst news sink in, pauses while processing, then somehow finds the perfect way to view it with an open heart and a hopeful view, glowing with radiant, positive light.

Hooper wasn't that guy.

He was the character who shut down when bad news was given. If this were a book of his, he would have written that scene much differently. Readers find it hard to get behind characters who shut down emotionally. Main characters who say mean, snarky things when people are trying to help them. There's not much to relate to, nothing to root for, little to hold on to as the pages flip by. Not much to keep the reader engaged. Unlikeable characters are just that—unlikeable. If the character has given up, then why shouldn't the reader?

Hooper was so unlikeable in that moment.

Some might argue he's been unlikeable in many of his moments.

Hooper opens his eyes, unaware he's still pacing the room. He thinks about calling the police. Walks through what that would look like. He'd call them, they'd come out, they'd ask him questions, and they'd find out who he is.

Worst case, one of the cops knows his books. It happens. Hooper's books have some of the most realistic cops in thrillers today, so he's been told. His series is a favorite among cops across the country because he *"gets it right."* Hooper has spent a lot of time with cops. Ride-alongs, cups of coffee, lunches, beers, and so on.

He stops. What if someone does recognize him? Not impossible. There's a strong chance someone would leak all this to the press. Vomit it all over the internet. Dear God, not Twitter.

Best-selling author visited by feral children in the woods.

Why is Nicholas Hooper alone in the woods?

What's he hiding from? Another bad relationship? More problems with the bottle?

Are those kids his?

Hooper shakes his head loose from the creative spiral of potentially harmful click-bait headlines. No one other than Allison and the doctors know anything about his condition—hates that word, *condition*. There has to be a way to take care of these kids while not blowing up what he's trying to do here.

Think...

There has to be a police station in that town with the good coffee. Looked to be a decent-sized yet small community. He could drive them to the station, slow down, and drop them off.

No. Allison's voice tears through his head. *Do better, you unbelievable asshole.*

Okay.

Take them to the police station, walk in with them, explain what he knows, but don't give them his name if he can avoid it. He can't avoid it. He's knows better. He'll have to give them a name. They'll ask for ID. He can lie. He'll do the fake pat-down of his person with a *how could I be so stupid* look of shock on his mug, then go with how he must have left his driver's license in his other jacket. Maybe sweet-talk the local, small-town PD.

Perhaps he'll wear a hat. Put in the contacts he hasn't jammed in his eyes in years. All the pictures of Hooper on the internet have him wearing his Lennon/Potter glasses. Also, wear clothes that don't look like page one of the pompous writer douchebag fall collection.

It's not that he's Brad Pitt or anything. The entire planet doesn't know him on sight, and if he has to give a name, he can use Nick Hooper.

He snaps his fingers. Even better, drop the Nicholas altogether and use his middle name. It's not CIA-level thinking, but it might be enough to get through this and somewhat do the right thing.

Hooper stops. Stands still while running it all back and forth through his mind once more. A mental proofread of the plan. They serve breakfast at the place with the coffee. Smelled pretty good. Those kids like food. He could take them there, load them up with pancakes or whatever, and get himself some of that good bean juice.

The girl is in charge, no question, so if he can get her on board with the pancakes, then it's good as done.

Hooper nods with smirk.

Snaps his fingers once again, so satisfied with himself.

"Everybody wins."

ELEVEN

THE GIRL SNUGGLES in close to her brother on the biggest couch she's ever seen.

A couch in the middle of the biggest house she's ever seen. Feels like a cozy, brown leather raft floating in a giant ocean.

The bright lights of the big, beautiful screen buzz and bump fun images. The speakers explode with the voices of one of her and her brother's favorites.

They used to sit on the floor at home watching for hours while their parents worked or did grown-up things. They'd stop and watch it with them even through the kids knew Mom and Dad probably didn't get it.

Her brother giggles.

She loves it when he giggles. Used to love

making him laugh. It hits her. This is the first time she's heard his laugh in a while.

First sound she's heard out of him in what seems like forever. They both just stopped talking. Something they did together. Both simply knew to stop. Ever since they were pulled out of their house that night. Thrown into the trunk of that mean man's car. The last thing her brother said to her was in the closet of their room. They were hiding. He asked her the one question she couldn't answer.

Are we going to die?

She's getting lost in the comfort of being on this couch. Distracted by how normal life is right this second, she lets her mind think that maybe things will be okay. This man who lives in this giant house seems like he's not bad, but she knows not to trust. Never trust an adult ever again.

Frakes pops into her mind. Standing with his hulking frame in the door of that shed with the moonlight peeking over the top of him. His thick rubber gloves slicked black with blood. She holds her brother tighter.

He giggles again, shoving a fistful of Cheetos into his mouth.

She's so tired. Eyes heavy like they're being

pulled down by bags of sand. Wants to sleep so bad but wants to stay awake to keep watch. She jerks herself free from drifting asleep, turning and looking behind the couch, checking the entryway and then the window for anything that might hurt them.

There's nothing there. Not yet at least.

She doesn't like that there's no door behind them, nothing to close, just an open space that leads to other parts of the house that they can't see in the darkness.

This place is too big. Too many places for bad people to hide. Makes her tense no matter how *not bad* this one man seems to be. Peeling herself off her brother, she gets up to take another peek.

There's a light on in a room down the hall. She can see the shadow of this maybe-not-bad man moving back and forth. Her brother giggles again, muffled through his full mouth.

Is this man planning something?

What is he going to do with us in this big house?

Her body feels as heavy as her eyes. Legs like concrete. Little cuts and scrapes burn here, there and everywhere. If he wanted to be bad, he probably would have done it by now. Maybe. Her shoulders inch up toward her ears.

Trust is earned, Mommy told her all the time.

Never given, Daddy would follow up.

Looking to her left toward the kitchen, she eyeballs a block of knives on the island. She slips over and pulls out the biggest one she can find, then tiptoes back over and climbs on the couch by her brother. He snuggles in, sharing the blanket as she slides the knife under the couch. Her shoulders inch back down, comforted by the fact the blade is at least nearby.

She leans her head on her brother's shoulder.

Finally allows her eyes to close.

TWELVE

FRAKES DRAGS himself in through the door.

Body reduced to heavy meat hanging off his bones.

He can barely see through his bleary, exhausted eyes. The morning sun cuts through the kitchen, slicing up the trash, the stacks of everything as flickers of dust hover above it all. A fly breaks in and out of the shafts of daylight like a Broadway star performing under the bright lights of the big stage.

Frakes has been at it all night.

Searching, tracking, hunting, looking for the boy and girl. Despite his best efforts, it did not bear fruit. His mind runs through all the possibilities he can think of. Where they are or what could have happened with them. Most of those possibilities are not good. If those kids are out on the loose, running free, free to talk to anyone, there's not a lot of great outcomes.

Almost none for Frakes or the master he serves.

A pot of coffee sits askew on the burner but still feels warm. Frakes opens the cabinet looking for his mug. It's one of the few gifts Mama ever gave him.

Nothing special, cheap item from a gift shop in town. A simple white mug with #1 Son in large black letters. It's the only cup he ever uses. Every morning he pours some coffee, making sure Mama sees him using her gift.

Moving boxes and various canisters out of the way, frustration mounts. He can't find the mug.

"Mama," he calls out, searching behind some other cups.

There's a noise from the other room. A thump. Sounds like a muffled voice.

Frakes pulls his gun from behind his back. Checks the load nice and quiet and readies the weapon with both hands, keeping his finger pressed to the side just off the trigger. He pushes through the kitchen door into the next room. He clears the corners. Trains the gun over the rest of the room.

It's empty.

No sign of anyone having been in here. One of the few clean, or somewhat clean, parts of the house.

Another thump.

Sounds like a cry. Maybe it's a laugh. There's a man's voice. All coming from Mama's room. The door is closed. She hardly ever shuts her door. It's kind of a rule of hers. *No closed doors in my house*, she used to say to him after catching him doing dirty things.

Frakes grips the gun tighter, moving his finger to the trigger.

The air in the house feels tight. Everything goes quiet. Only that big, old clock that Mama loves ticks behind him. His heart pounds. His mind whips to the kids.

Someone found them. Everything is wrong. Broken. It's all falling apart.

The door flies open.

Out steps a tall man with tats running from his wrists to his jawline. Sweat beads along his bald head. He owns hard eyes that end conversations. A line of sweat breaks, running down from his temple across his bare chest.

He holds a mug that says #1 Son.

"Well? You going to use that?" The man

pushes his chin toward the gun. "Or are you just kinda screwing around?"

"No, Hauk." Frakes lowers his gun. "I didn't—"

"Didn't what, exactly?" Hauk wipes the sweat clear from his face. Snaps the elastic of his boxers while flashing a whiplash smile. "Didn't know I was stopping by?"

Frakes sees Mama pulling on her dress behind Hauk in her bedroom. The bed is a mess. Sheets wadded up on the floor. A white-hot ball forms in Frakes's stomach. His anger pulse thumps harder than ever.

"Nothing." Frakes looks away as fast as he can.

"Damn right, nothing." Hauk circles, speaking down to Frakes as his hard eyes dig. "Your poor mama calls me all upset in the dead of night asking for help and you do what? Show up the next morning, out all night, with a gun in hand? That sound cool to you?"

Mama steps out from her room lighting up a smoke with her ever-present hand torch. A satisfied smile spread wide. Frakes can't even look her in the eye. He knows that goofy smile. Hates the look she gets when Hauk comes to visit. Hauk hands her the mug. Mama takes it, takes a sip, swishes the coffee around in her mouth.

Frakes keep his eyes on his mug. His gift. His flesh burns.

"I..." Frakes fights for what to say. "I was out looking for something."

"You don't say."

"I told him, son," Mama pipes in, blowing smoke over Hauk's shoulder. "Told him what happened. What you done."

Frakes raises his eyes to meet hers. He can't believe it. He looks to the bed, then back to the mug. His sight flashes to white as the pulse takes over. The entire world starts to bend and weave.

Hauk raises Frakes's chin between his finger and thumb, forcing him to meet his stare. The muscles in Hauk's jaw clench. Veins in his neck bulge like fat worms under his inked skin.

Hauk raises a balled fist.

Frakes steps back but doesn't cower. He plants his feet, all his weight on the back foot. Slips his gun back into his dirty jeans.

There's a click in his head.

They are about the same height, but Frakes has Hauk by fifty pounds or so. They've never fought before, but Frakes has seen Hauk deliver some beatings. Hauk has seen Frakes deliver more than a few as well. Frakes knows what Hauk can do to someone, not to mention what the crew of deranged psychos Hauk has at his command can do to a person. If they are told to.

Some might say Frakes is one of those deranged psychos.

Some might argue Frakes is the best, and worst, of them.

"You're all right, Frakes." Hauk lowers his fist, breaking into a thunderous laugh. "Your boss shows up, bangs your mom, and you want to fight." He shrugs, then finds his pants on the floor. "Can understand that, of course. Life gets weird as hell, don't it?"

Frakes goes back to staring at the mug in Mama's hand.

"Problem is, you did something Full-on Frakes. Something I do not understand. Can you take a minute? Explain your actions to me?"

Frakes starts to speak.

Hauk puts up a finger. "Now, I do want you to tell me all about it, but please, make it so a simple boy like me can understand." He lowers his finger, takes the # 1 Son mug from Mama. "Talk slow. Small words if you could."

"You know what happened, Hauk."

"I do?" Slurps the coffee. "Well, I know some of it, sure."

"Little more than some."

"You getting smart with me? That what you're doing?" Hauk steps in close, eye to eye. "I said tell me about it. What did you do?"

Frakes is calm and cold on the outside. Inside, kerosene flows through his veins, only needing a tiny spark to ignite. The tips of his fingers tingle, longing for the grip of his gun.

"Or rather, what didn't you do?"

Now, Frakes offers his own smile. "Well, I didn't kill those kids."

Mama looks down, shaking her head in a show of exaggerated shame.

Hauk nods, takes a step back. Frakes knows damn well that Mama told him everything already. Hauk is just being the boss. Doing what bosses do around here. Frakes has worked for him for years, seen this tactic before with others, so Frakes knows the math on conversations like this.

Hauk will want a pound of flesh for his ledger. There will be a debt to pay.

"Never knew you to be so soft, sir." Hauk hands the coffee mug back to Mama.

There's a knock at the door.

Frakes yanks his gun free, leveled on the door in a snap.

"Easy there, Full-on Frakes," Hauk says. "Called an officer of the peace in on this."

Frakes keeps his gun out. The idea that Tipton is out there doesn't make him feel any better. Opening the door, he finds Tipton leaning on the side of the house. A cool breeze rushes in, taking some of the heat away from Frakes's face and body.

"May I?" Tipton motions inside.

"Come on in, buddy," Hauk booms from the living room. "Just chatting some this morning."

Tipton pushes past Frakes into the house.

"Why don't you go on and make us some of that delightful breakfast casserole thing you always do. Love it." Hauk gives Mama a little spank. "Go on now."

Mama jolts forward, licking her lips as she slinks off into the kitchen. With his jaw tight like a vice, Frakes watches his mug go into the kitchen with her.

"Now, Officer Tipton." Hauk offers him a seat on the beat-up, puke-green couch. "We were just discussing an employee-and-employer issue."

"Were you now?" Tipton takes a seat. "Frakes mess something up?"

"He did indeed."

Hauk points at the couch, indicating that Frakes should have a seat and take his talking-to. Frakes thinks about doing something, not sure what, thinks better of it, eventually takes a seat next to Tipton. Decides standing versus sitting down isn't the battle to fight. He keeps his gun resting on his knee, however.

Hauk walks back and forth in front of the couch, eyes glued on Frakes as if he's a young boy being lectured about household chores.

"We have a problem. Our man Frakes here took it upon himself to deviate and now we have a real mess on our hands." Hauk stops. "That fair to say, Frakes?"

Frakes stares back.

"What?" Tipton scratches his head. "What the hell happened?"

"You remember that thing a little while back? With that house and the kids?"

"I do."

"Well, Frakes here took it upon himself to take in some strays."

"Huh?"

"Wanted to start a little family, I guess."

"That's not it." Frakes fires up from the

couch, his gun hanging by his side. "You know damn well what happened."

"Sit. Your big. Dumb ass. Down." Every muscle in Hauk's body is coiled tight.

Frakes takes a seat.

"And you better put that gun away before you do more stupid shit you can't handle." Hauk begins moving back and forth again. "Now, back to the situation at hand."

Frakes slips the gun behind his back. Tipton watches, shaking his head, making sure Hauk sees his disgust.

"These kids are now on the loose. Fled this happy little home." Hauk looks around the dirty walls and busted-up furniture. "Can't imagine why."

"This is a shithole," Tipton adds.

"Facts. You speak facts." Hauk points to Tipton. "You also need to find facts. I need you to get on this shit. Ask around. Check with your people. They heard anything about two kids roaming around. Anybody called something in."

"Roger that." Tipton nods. "We got a description of these kids? Which way they went?"

The sound of Hauk and Tipton talking fades into the background like a dirty, disgusting form of white noise. Frakes's thoughts turn to the boy and girl.

Running around in the woods. Alone. Probably scared to death. Maybe they're lost or even hurt on the side of some back road.

Maybe they've already found the cops. Of course, if they'd found the cops, Tipton would have probably heard about it already. Besides, if that news somehow made it past Tipton, the Feds would be storming this house this very second. But Frakes can't let Hauk and his people find those kids either. It's not right. Not after what they've done to those kids' parents.

Not after what Frakes has done.

Frakes looks to Tipton, then to Hauk.

Wants to claw his own flesh off the bone. This tickle of hate is morphing fast into a spreading, burning ripple effect. He wants to rip the smug look off Tipton's face and shove it down Hauk's throat. His stampeding mind runs with the thought. He can almost hear Tipton's guttural screams while holding the exposed meat of his face, then the chunky noises of Hauk choking, gagging for air while Frakes pushes his fist farther and farther down.

Hauk snaps his fingers an inch from Frakes's eyes.

"Come back. Join us." Hauk has his hands planted on his knees, leaning down. "You mind telling Officer Tipton here what those kids look like? Perhaps a direction they might be traveling?"

Frakes slicks back his few remaining hairs and offers up the thinnest of smiles.

"One is a girl. One is a boy. No earthly idea which way they went."

THIRTEEN

HOOPER SITS across from the children.

The small-town diner smells of breakfast heaven. Coffee, syrup, bacon all mixed together floating through the air, engulfing them like a hug given by an angel.

The red vinyl booth gives a dull rub-squeak as children lean forward and then back, digging into plates of pancakes that are bigger than their faces. There's an old-school bell on the front door that gives a soft but audible ding as people come and go. Made Hooper nuts at first, but after a few minutes, it's become part of the soundtrack to the place.

He asked the children if they wanted to shower or anything before they left the house. The girl shook her head and the boy, of course, said nothing as well. They both still look like they were raised in a dumpster, but he did manage to talk them into taking a damp cloth to their faces. Took some extra effort, but he also convinced them to remove the dried Cheeto dust from their hands.

Last night went better than Hooper thought it would.

The children crashed hard after about six and a half episodes of SpongeBob. Both curled up like baby kittens on that cushy couch in the living room. Hooper found a blanket and some pillows from one of the multiple bedrooms. Did his best to position them so they at least looked comfortable.

Hooper slept on a couch in the game room. Didn't think he should be too far away from them in case they woke up in the middle of the night. Thought it was the adult thing to do. That's a lie. Well, not completely. He did worry that these children who are on the run, in a strange house, might be prone to nightmares, but the complete truth is Hooper wasn't ready for sleep in that huge house all alone. At least not upstairs, which is more or less like a whole separate house. A fact he didn't realize until he walked upstairs to the massive master bedroom for the first time.

There's a crushing quiet in that house. So quiet, it amps up the voices in his head. Makes them louder than hell, especially at night. And those voices had a lot to say.

Talk of conditions, meds, unwritten books, upset sisters, and oh yeah, wayward children. Scary questions about... well, anything and everything.

Never realized the sounds of New York—the sirens, the occasional nonsense shouting, honking cars—provided him with the white noise lullaby to drown out the conversational rat-tat that works his mind over almost constantly. But this brand of quiet in the woods? It creeps him the hell out. Hooper hardly slept at all.

The bell at the diner's door dings its welcoming ding.

The music of the day is an enchanting mix of soft rock from the seventies and early eighties. Pretty sure he caught some Juice Newton on the way in.

Hooper feels the tension in every part of his body. Each molecule pulled together in unforgiving balls of anxiety. Even here with the wonderful smells of small-town breakfast, Juice Newton and the rest, his thoughts stab at him like an ice pick.

The idea of going to the police. The thought of turning these kids over to the cops without knowing what is going to happen to them has Hooper twisted in ways he didn't think were possible.

Obviously, he's not the right guy to help them, but still, they aren't stray puppies in a cardboard box. Maybe he'll ask the cops to keep him informed. Give him updates. Let him know that their parents or legal guardian have been found. Give him some form of happy ending to tuck away so he can get on with things. Hooper embraces the selfish need to feel better about all this.

He wishes the girl and boy would tell him something.

Anything.

Hell, they haven't looked at him since the burly waiter dropped them off at this table. The man's thick forearms had LUV tattooed on one arm and HATE on the other. Hooper made a mental note—then tapped it into his phone to make sure he got it. A pretty cool little nugget he could use in a book later.

Sipping his coffee—can't get over how good it is—Hooper watches the kids attack the pancakes with much more aggression than the Cheetos.

Watching joy creates joy. Comforting to know that no matter what brand of horrible these kids are going through those pancakes can still cut through. That joy sits on the top of his thoughts for only a moment before it melts away.

He thinks of the tattoos on the man's arms. The note on his phone. Hooper's heart skips a beat. He might not get a chance to use that little gem. Might not be around to write another book.

The door dings.

Pulling his phone, he deletes the note. As he sets his phone down, his hands begin to tremble. He grips them together tight. Teeth grinding, he locks his fingers together until their color cycles from pink to red to purple. Shakes them hard, loosens his grip, wiggles his fingers. Closes his eyes, searching to find his breathing. The sound of clicking forks on plates gives him a rhythm to work with. Something for him to focus on. A scrap of wood to cling to in a raging sea. As his heartbeat returns to some semblance of normal, he starts to feel his hands holding steady.

Doctor warned him of moments like this one. There are pills to help with some of this. Pills for other things too. Meds to push back against a body that's betraying him. Going back on a deal Hooper thought they had made long ago. Body and mind in this together. The Hooper premium package. Body, mind and soul walking between the raindrops while the rest of world marvels at how damn cool we are.

All together now, with feeling, let's do this thing called life...

He opens his eyes.

The clicks and clacks of forks have stopped. The children are watching him from across the table. Their patented blank stares working overtime. Syrup flung on like paint clings to the sides of their faces while chewing with extended chipmunk cheeks. Hooper puts on a fake smile.

"Good stuff?" Gives a gameshow host wave to the almost empty plates in front of them. "Enjoy the eats?"

The boy nods fast and furious. The most emotional response he's seen out of the boy. He goes back to the work of pancakes. The girl gives a single nod but still keeps her eyes on Hooper. Her expression has shifted to something Hooper hasn't seen from either of them yet.

Concern.

There's a look of honest concern on the girl's face. She must have seen all that. Seen the anxiety show Hooper put on across the table. No way she missed the entire mini-meltdown he just had. Makes a mental note—one he already suspected—the girl is sharp as hell.

"I'm fine." He puts both hands up. "It's fine."

He picks up the phone, finishes deleting all the notes he's put in there. *What's the point?*

Life is through the windshield, not the rearview mirror, his mother told him once after Hooper asked a question about his dad's death. Hooper had asked if she missed him. Allison wanted to know too. Their mother started to answer but stopped, coughed into her hand, allowing only the beginnings of a tear, then gave them that pithy yet memorable nugget. She did mutter something about life being an imperfect time for everyone. Such an odd, yet delicious response.

Hooper had apologized, not sure why. He was still a child, but he always did this hat-in-hand apologetic sort of thing, then dragged himself into his and his sister's room when their mother shut down like that. Mom didn't like to talk about it.

Hooper never asked her why, but he and Allison always assumed it simply hurt too much to discuss. Their mother thought putting on a show of being strong was better than crying all the time. Maybe she was right. Sometimes she'd buy them something, if she could pull together enough money, but the strangeness of not talking about their dad always stuck with Hooper.

Their mother always had sound words after those times. The life/windshield bit was one of her better ones, but what if your windshield was showing you a brick wall out in the distance and that brick wall was getting closer and closer? Holding your breath, knowing impact is certain. The only thing between you and those bricks is time and distance. What if all you have left is what's in the rearview?

A tremor rattles his hands again. The girl places her tiny hand on his.

Hooper looks up.

The girl's eyes are locked into him. Wide, warm, without judgement as she holds her soft grip on the tops of his shaking hands. She tilts her head left as if saying, *You're full of shit, old man. You're soooo not fine.* Hooper may have projected some of his own thoughts to what she might be thinking, but the bones of it are there.

"Too much coffee." Hooper slips his hands out from under hers. Takes a sip of his now favorite coffee and holds his cup out for Mr. Luv/Hate to give him a refill. "Gets me all jittery sometimes."

The girl pulls her hands back under the table.

There's a ding at the front door.

"I'm going to visit the bathroom. You guys going to be okay?"

The girl drops her fork.

Body goes stiff. Eyes zeroed in on the door. She's the one trembling now. The boy turns to her, then whips around to the door. His lips quiver. Shakes his head no as his eyes swell.

"What?" Hooper places his palms on the table, leaning in. "What's wrong?"

The girl points with a trembling hand toward the door, then pulls it back quickly as if the open air were a hot stove.

There's a skinny, wiry police officer standing at the front counter talking to the woman working the register. They are laughing and yapping as if they've known each other for years.

Hooper glances at the cop, then back to the children. They are terrified.

"Do you know him?" Hooper keeps his voice low. "Do you know that policeman?"

She nods hard, her eyes wide and watery.

"Go," she says.

"Why? What is—"

"Go. Now."

He's never seen a more complete shift in someone, child or adult, from the youthful bliss of a plate of pancakes to absolute terror. Other than the word *help*, these are the only other words she's said to him.

Go. Now.

Hooper mouths a silent okay, then turns to the boy.

"Do you want to leave too?"

The boy closes his eyes tight, nodding as tears roll down his cheeks.

"Okay. Okay. Let's get the hell out of here."

The girl places her hands back on his. Hooper nods, waiting for her to lead the way. The girl points to the back of the diner, away from the cop at the door. She and the boy push down, staying low in the booth as if trying to stay out of sight of the cop at the front.

"Out the back?" Hooper looks toward the cop. Best he can tell, the cop hasn't looked their way, still chatting up the woman at the counter. "Okay. I guess we can get out that way. Not sure there's an exit for customers, but—"

The girl digs her nails into his hand.

"Got it. Go and now."

Hooper slides out from the booth, tossing way too much cash on the table while using his body to shield the view of cop from the kids as they climb out from the booth. The kids move fast toward the back of the diner. Dodging locals, weaving between waitstaff balancing trays of food. To everyone else, they seem like unruly children rather than the truth. Hooper shrugs when a woman gives him a *discipline your kids* look.

Turning back toward the front of the diner, Hooper stops cold.

The cop is looking his way.

Dead at Hooper. The two men lock eyes. Only for a moment, but enough for Hooper to feel a chill deep in his bones. Looking away as fast as he can, he sees the girl waving him on. Luckily, there's an exit by the bathrooms that seems like it's out of view from the front. The girl holds the door open, clearly not happy that Hooper is taking his sweet time.

Moving with purpose, Hooper heads to the back but doesn't want to rush. Doesn't want to bring any unnecessary attention to himself. He's pretty sure the cop isn't coming his way or following him, but he did not like the look of that guy. Beady eyes. Small-town skinny cop with something to prove written all over him.

Hooper can feel the cop's stare.

Got those scanning, searching cop eyes. Semi-lifeless but breaking down the situation at all times. Maybe Hooper is being paranoid, understandable given that mysterious children showed up at his door and are now terrified at the sight of the police officer, but there was something to what just happened. This feeling rocketing through Hooper is real. He knows cops. Met a lot of them while working on his books.

That one at the door, he wasn't just on the job.

There was something else going on behind those cop eyes.

FOURTEEN

THE GIRL and boy head straight to the couch.

Laser-targeted missiles seeking comfort in an animated sponge.

Hooper watches them as he locks the door and puts on the chain. He'd changed the channel this morning to see if the news mentioned anything about missing kids in the area.

Those kids knew where to find their favorite channel. Went right to it. There was no pause, no searching. They knew where it was without a hint of hesitation. Hooper takes note.

Maybe they memorized it from last night. Not out of the question, but maybe they didn't. What if they already knew what channel they loved and where to find it on the menu? If they know the channels, then it's possible they are local or at least from close by. At least within the radius of the cable lineup. He tucks that information away while his mind works over that cop at the diner.

The look he had on his face.

The way he zeroed in on him. The way the girl and boy reacted at the mere sight of him. Hooper isn't sure if the cop saw them or not, but he was there for a reason. Asking the cashier a lot of questions while pouring on his small-town lawman charm. He was looking for someone. Or multiple someones.

Hooper has never claimed to be a mathematical genius, but if you add together those cop eyes and the terrified eyes of the children, you get a sum of something that is seriously wrong here. Perhaps they are just two kids who ran away from home and the local PD is trying to get them back to their parents, who are worried sick about them. Again, not out of the question and perfectly reasonable.

Also not a stretch to consider that Hooper's highly skilled, highly paid imagination is getting the best of him.

All the thrillers he's written. All the crime he's studied—real and imaginary—has been spinning inside his brain for most of his adult life.

Most normal humans don't think of crime and how to get away with it day after day.

Am I making too much of this?

Is this not as sinister as I'm making it out to be in my writer/medicated mind?

All that is possible too.

But this feels different to Hooper. Hard to describe—and not to be flaky about it, but there is a vibe to all this that feels way off. Way more than kids who got lost or ran away because they weren't allowed to stay up late or whatever. And there is one huge question that stands in the center of Hooper's mind waving its arms wildly and calling out for an answer.

Why were those kids so scared of that cop?

"What the hell are you doing?"

Hooper drops his keys. His lungs and heart stop functioning. So in his own head he didn't even hear his sister come inside.

Allison stands in the kitchen stabbing at the air, pointing at the kids on the couch. Her confused, borderline-enraged face crunched up in a ball and shifting to a new shade of red with each passing second. Her hands are raised, held in a perfect position to strangle her brother.

Hooper holds his chest, making sure his heart is still there. Then, in hopes of peaceful communication, he tilts his head, aiming it back down the hall, silently suggesting a better place to have this conversation. The short walk will also buy Hooper some precious seconds to come up with what to say.

They move quiet and quick into the game room with Allison leading the way. Hooper closes the door behind them, creating as little noise as possible. Sucking in a deep breath, he turns, spins rather, into a talk show host stance.

Allison takes two fast steps to the center of the room and stops, eyes wide, arms held out wide as if waiting for answers to fall from the sky. Cloaked in disbelief, she turns in a half circle, moving along with the gears grinding inside her mind. Trying to manufacture some understanding. Hooper thumbs toward the bar, hoping a drink might help things, even if it is still considered too early for most stable people.

"No," she whisper-screams.

Hooper pours himself one.

"Fine," she relents, whipping her wrist back and forth toward the bottle as a yes. "What the hell is going on? Why are there two children in this house?"

"Fascinating story, actually."

"Who are they?"

"I don't know."

Hooper hands her a glass. They both take the drinks down in one gulp.

"Do better," she says, wiping her lip.

"They just showed up. They showed up at the front door not long after you left. I tried to tell you. I called you, dammit, and tried—"

"You didn't try to tell me shit. You were a distant dickhead waiting for me to pick and pull information out of you like the child you always are."

"Now, to be fair, you were a little dismissive. Let's agree on that. I had a real problem and you—"

"Didn't want to hack through your fresh crop of one-liner bullshit to get to the point."

"But it was an emergency, as you can plainly see."

"You should have opened with *there are two children on my couch, Allison.*"

Hooper stops his mouth from saying something he'll regret. She's right. Telling her that on the phone would have been more effective, but he sees no reason to give her an edge in this conversation.

"What do we do?" He takes her empty glass, heading back to the bar.

"We?"

"Of course. You are here, right?"

Hooper turns back to her with two fresh glasses of the good stuff. Only filled a little higher this time. Allison has become very quiet and very still. Jaw clenched. Eyes full. This always terrifies Hooper.

"What?" Hooper sets the drinks down. "Look, I know this is nuts but... why did you come back, anyway?"

"I..." She hesitates, almost disgusted with herself. "I came back because you sounded like you were in trouble. And, dammit, I'm glad I did."

"Look. I know we—"

Allison pulls his gun from behind her back.

The .357 that was given to Hooper. The one that resided in a silk pillowcase. She found it. He hates himself for being stupid enough to leave it on the dining room table next to the front door.

"What is this for?" She holds the gun flat in her palm gently, like an egg. "You get how messed up this looks, right? You call me, get me worried, I come back to find you've got a gun and children."

"There's a lot to unpack here."

"Begin with the gun."

"Thought I might need it out here. You know? Hanging out in the wild and all that."

With her free hand, she removes from her pocket the one bullet he packed for the trip.

"Do better."

Hooper looks away and shrugs. Not much to say. No way to say it anyway.

"Talk." She closes her fingers around the bullet. "Tell me what is happening. What were you planning to do up here?"

"It's not what you think."

"Oh? Looks a lot like you came up here to blow your brains out."

"Not my style."

"Not your style. What? You're more of a fist-ful-of-pills kind of guy? The gun was just so you had a colorful option?"

"Stop." Hooper takes a drink. "Can we discuss the children?"

Allison wipes away a tear before it becomes an all-out cry, then shoves the bullet back deep into her pocket while slipping the gun behind her back. A move she must have learned while attending the guns-and-weapons training sessions she and Hooper went to during various research trips. There was the group of former SEALs in San Diego that put on a class last year for Hollywood types and out-of-shape writers. Also, there was the high-end personal protection agency in Miami that gave them a special one-on-one session, and of course, the countless nights and weekends doing ride-alongs with cops and detectives in New York and LA.

Hooper personally hates all the violence. Loves writing about it, but dislikes being that close to it. The reality of it makes his stomach turn.

Allison took it all in stride. Didn't love it either, but she absorbed it as a necessary evil in an evil world. A line she told him. A line he used in countless books. For the record, he always gave her credit in the Acknowledgments section at the back. One she claims nobody ever reads.

"Only you would change the subject of your suicide to why there are two children in your rented mansion."

"I do hate boring."

Allison coughs an unwanted laugh through her restrained tears.

"Well, sister Allison." Hooper hands her a fresh glass. "What in the sweet hell do we do?"

FIFTEEN

"DID YOU EVEN TRY THE POLICE?"

"Sort of." Hooper sips his bourbon this time. No reason to get all sloppy this early in the day. There are children here for God's sake. "*Try* is the right word, however."

"Need you to put some meat on the bone, bro."

"I took them into town with the intention of going to the police."

"Good. And?" She stretches *and* into a three-syllable word.

"And we stopped to have some pancakes at the place I told you about with the great coffee I found and—"

"Damn nice of you. Focus. Cops. Children."

"That's the thing. We were having pancakes

and this local cop walked into the diner." Hooper's faces slumps. His wiseass nature drifts. "They were terrified. You should have seen them. The second they saw him."

"What do you mean?"

"It's like they knew the cop. Froze up at the sight of him. They couldn't get away fast enough. As if the devil strolled in for breakfast."

"What did they say?"

Hooper goes to the door and peeks out, checking on the kids. They are still planted on the couch soaking up the television. They did grab themselves the bag of Cheetos, he notices.

"Hooper. What did they say?"

"Oh. They don't talk."

"Pardon?"

"They do not speak. Well, the girl does a little, but the boy doesn't say shit." Hooper slips over to Allison, getting close just in case the kids can hear. "Something has happened to them, Allison. I don't know what, but I'm guessing it is something really, really bad. I mean, why would two kids their age be wandering around in the woods? They were all alone at night, and then they go catatonic at the sight of a cop?"

Allison nods, soaking in everything he's saying.

Hooper knows he did his job and presented the information. He can see his sister's big brain churning through all the horrific possibilities. Ones Hooper has had more time to sift through.

They both have poured over true crime data, countless police case files, demented Google searches, all in the name of story research over the years. Both know the fiction of the dark side of life is no match for the reality of the human experience.

"Can you reach out to some people?" Hooper asks.

"You thinking Ross or Dutch?"

"Them or anyone else you can think of. Good people, though. Ones who don't blab around. Tell them I'm researching a new book—children on the run type of thing—but see if they can dump the databases around here in this area. Anything about any missing children. Boy and a girl around their ages. Recently, like in the last month or two. More like in the last week or two."

Hooper knows Allison is already at least five steps ahead of him. She's more than likely already mapped out who to call and what to say. She'll do calls rather than email. No record, or less chance of a record at least. She has some deep ties with some very discreet detectives, both active and retired, and they are paid well for their knowledge, expertise and the before-mentioned discretion.

Not to mention, they signed some white-shoe, New York lawyer NDAs that will go wrath of God on those who blab about the work of Nicholas Hooper. Can't have those multimillion-dollar plotlines leaking out on social media or any other bullshit.

"On it." Allison takes down the rest of her drink. "Please, don't do anything stupid."

"Look who you're talking to."

"Serious. Do not be an idiot. You're a writer, not a hero. A sick one at that."

She didn't mean it as a sucker punch, but it sure as hell felt like one.

Hooper hasn't thought about any of that since they got back from pancakes. Now it all floods back in. The schedule of pills races through his head. The spreadsheet that Allison put together for him. The breathing exercises he knows will help him but won't do. Seems like he's been holding his breath ever since he talked to that doctor.

"You hear me, bro?"

Hooper shoves all of it aside as if pulling back

the stage curtain, revealing his patented smile with his wire-rimmed glasses.

"Everything's fine."

Allison jams her tongue into her cheek to keep her from biting it off.

He extends his arm, offering her an exit to the game room. Slipping back down the hall toward the living room, Hooper has his eyes on the backs of the children's heads. They are still sharing Cheetos, giggling at the goofy fun up on the screen that's almost too big for the wall it hangs on.

Hooper glances out the window to the left of the living room. The trees go as deep as the eye can see. The sun lighting a picture-perfect day. Nothing but lush greens, blue skies, and take-your-breath-away mountains.

What happened to these kids?

In this perfect spot, in the middle of all this beauty, what happened to this little girl and boy?

Hooper clears his throat. "Kids." The girl and boy turn around. "This is my sister, Allison. She's leaving but she'll be back. You'll probably see her around—"

"Hi, Allison," the boy says.

"What the hell?" Hooper's eyes pop wide.

The boy. He spoke. To her, never to me.

The girl's little hand waves a hello.

"Hi," Allison says, cute and warm. "It's very nice to meet you." Allison wraps her arm around Hooper, giving his shoulder a hard slap-slap. "Take care of this guy for me while I'm gone. Do you mind? He's a mess but he's okay when it counts. You know the type, right?"

The girl giggles, giving a thumbs-up.

The boy agrees with a single, solid confirming nod.

Allison bounces her eyebrows at Hooper, making sure he knows the kids like her better. The kids turn their attention back to SpongeBob. Hooper stands with feet planted, still shell-shocked that the boy spoke to her. He was borderline bubbly about it too.

"I'll call," Allison says before closing the door behind her.

Hooper drops down into the ridiculously comfortable chair next to the couch. The mid-morning bourbon is starting to loosen his mind a little.

He hopes Allison finds something. Anything that will help.

He can't keep them here forever, but where to go with this is as fuzzy as what's happened to these kids. Allison's contacts will move quick.

She'll know something soon, maybe even later today or tomorrow. Still, it can't be soon enough. Struggling to keep his paranoia at bay, he thinks of what they might be running from. Why the cops might be an enemy to them.

The front door opens.

Hooper almost peels out of his own skin.

Allison pokes her head in, waving Hooper to come over to her at the door. Pulling himself up from the chair, he drags his tired bones across the room. Allison removes the single bullet from her pocket. She holds it in front of Hooper's face. Its gold casing catches the sunlight perfectly to match the moment.

"Just so we're clear. I'm taking these with me." She removes the gun from behind her back, waving it back and forth. "Not safe. You know, with children in the house."

She closes the door.

Hooper can't help but be impressed by the burn his sister just laid on him.

The kids giggle. He thinks for a second they caught all that, but they didn't. They are deep in the hypnotic pull of the screen.

Hooper closes his eyes, breathes in, counts, then breathes out. Then repeats once more. His mind clears, not completely, but his head is less jumbled than it was a minute ago. A simple breathing exercise they told him about at the hospital during an introductory appointment. Hates to admit it's doing some good. Opening his eyes, he focuses on the woods and sunshine outside. The possible good in the world just beyond the glass. The world that is still here. One he's still a part of.

At least now there's a semblance of a plan. An outline of something that might form the beginnings of an end.

His phone buzzes. Hooper shakes his head in semi-disgust. Allison loaded an app on his phone while he wasn't looking. She talked about it, he refused, but it looks like she did it anyway.

The app goes off in accordance with Hooper's medication schedule. Funny, it's as if she knew the spreadsheet wouldn't be enough. There's a part of him that appreciates that someone still gives a shit about him, but there is another thick slice of him that wishes no one did.

A flutter of nausea started a few minutes ago —didn't want to draw attention to it—along with a dull pain that began to thump away at his temples. He's getting to where he can almost tell it's time for his meds before any app or spreadsheet tells him. Hooper taps his phone, temporarily snoozing the app.

As he fills a glass of water, he pulls out the hated pill case from inside his duffle bag. Not lost on him that he still hasn't unpacked. The see-through blue case with a cartoon lion—Allison's touch—holds all the scientific means to keep him somewhat comfortable and stave off what he's been told is inevitable.

Well, no one said his demise was inevitable, but it was heavily implied. There was loose talk of new procedures, but none of them sounded like anything fun he'd like to try anytime soon. And much like with the super real estate agent, Hooper tuned out during most of it.

He's done his best to stay off the internet; the worst thing a person can do when diagnosed is scour the internet. Anything beyond a papercut, stay with the doctors. Yet, he couldn't stay away completely.

The lure of information, as false as most of it may be, was too much to avoid. Too easy to find what you want to hear or destroy any hope you may have about anything. Hooper found every-thing from confirmation the doctors are completely correct, to it is all a conspiracy to prop up big pharma so don't listen to anything the doctors say. Some say just drink a half-gallon mixture of cayenne pepper and lemon juice twice a day, and oh yeah, pray a lot.

Hooper takes the first fistful of pills.

His father died of something similar.

Different name, same variety, and he was a little older than Hooper is now but not by much. Hooper has devoted his life to not living like his father. Family man. Company man. Good guy who got run over by larger guys for most of his shortened life. Hooper fought all of it tooth and nail, only to end up in the same place.

History may not repeat itself entirely, but it's got the same rhythm, his dad told him once.

All the therapists, plus all the wives, have told him pieces of this anti-father narrative. How transparent Hooper is in his desire to not be his dad. Some were dead on, early on in the relationship. Those were the quickest to end, oddly enough. Hooper is certain there's no connection.

The pills slide down his throat. Lumps of bio-engineering traveling down deep into his gut. He imagines them dissolving into some form of amazing show of lights and music inside of him. His body giving their contents a hero's welcome. They've come to save him after all. Hero pills down the hatch to right the wrongs.

The kids giggle again.

What happened to you kids?

What are you running from?

No question, they can't stay here forever. He's not a complete asshole, but he's not Santa either. He wants to help, but he also would like to get on with the not writing of the book he came out here to write.

The book no one wants to read, at least not from him. The one that would end his career, or at least begin the question of whether the great Nicholas Hooper has lost a step or not. Of course, if he's dead, then it will sell a billion copies because that's just how shit works.

They will call it a dying man's masterpiece. His last message to us all. No matter how big of a pile of shit it is. That's the beauty of this little plan. There's no downside to Hooper. He'll be long gone when the dipshit vultures come around to pick apart his work.

A writer's dream.

The girl turns around, looking back at him. A quiet moment between them. A silent transference of some sort. As if they are firing off questions at one another without speaking. Hooper wants to rush over and shake the girl and boy both. Nothing crazy, just enough to jar loose a word or more. Some sort of explanation. It's the fumbling wondering that kills him.

The girl cracks some of a smile.

Hooper does the same, raising his glass of water in a kind of toast. The girl raises a Cheeto. The boy snatches it away from her. The girl holds her gaze on Hooper, shaking her head, pretending to be mad at her brother and the lost snack.

She mouths a silent *Thank you*.

Hooper shrugs. Takes everything he has to be cool in this moment.

The girl shrugs too, releasing the remainder of her smile, then turns back to SpongeBob and her Cheeto-thief of a brother.

Hooper considers popping some more of his hero pills.

SIXTEEN

"IT HAD TO BE THEM. Not a single doubt in my mind."

Tipton storms into the house, whipping the front door closed behind him.

Frakes and Mama's house shakes off the hard clap of the slamming door. Tipton's wiry frame buzzes with excitement like a dog that's brought back an amazing stick. Talking fast, using his hands, his words fight each other to race out of his mouth.

"There was a guy. Not local. Looked New York, Wall Street asshole or something like that. Must be renting a place here."

Hauk's head gives a series of quick nods, running his tongue over his teeth.

"You saw them?" There's an unmistakable

layer of relief to Frakes's voice. More wanting than hunting. "You sure about that?"

Hauk looks Frakes over, eyes searching and searing.

They've been sitting in this run-down shitbox of a domicile for too long. It's taking a toll on Hauk. His tight muscles pop under his skin as he presses hard on the top of his head. As if pushing on his brain will deliver the answers to a question he hasn't asked. Not out loud at least.

"Did you see them?" Hauk asks.

"Those kids?" Tipton asks.

"Yes." Hauk can't believe he has to clarify. "Did you see the boy and the girl?"

"Didn't see them. No. Someone said they might have seen some kids with him, though. But I'm telling you, that guy, the New York guy, he was jittery as hell. Had those eyes, ya know?"

"*Might* have seen kids with him? *Eyes*? What eyes?" Frakes looks to Hauk, then back to Tipton. "That what we're doing now? Eyes?"

"Eyes tell you a lot, Frakes. *Windows to the soul* as the blah-blah goes." Hauk pulls back a rag posing as a curtain, checking outside. "A person's peepers tell me all kinds of shit."

"Listen to me, man." Tipton impressed with himself. "That guy is hiding something. Didn't look like some dude enjoying a sit-down breakfast on vacation or whatever."

Hauk presses him. "A cop shows up at a diner eyeballing the hell out of him. Most people don't relax."

"True. True enough, I get that, but you got to trust me on this one."

"Trust you." Frakes moves in quick. Tipton stutter-steps in reverse. Backs up an inch from the wall. "You mean trust you like with that house?"

"Been through all that, man." Tipton looks away. "Said I was sorry. How many times I gotta say it?"

"Sorry?" Frakes balls his fists. Anger pulse pounding.

"We made it right, Frakes." Tipton looks for support. "Right, Hauk? We made that shit right, then Frakes here didn't do what needed to be done."

Frakes sees white.

His mind a bonfire in a snap. Pulls his massive fist back behind his ear before he even knows he's doing it. Hauk's arm locks onto his, hooking him at the elbow and spinning him around to face Hauk.

Nose to nose.

"It happens." Hauk's voice is cold and even. "It was a mess, sure, but messes do indeed happen. Much like the mess you've made, Frakes."

"What we did was wrong, Hauk."

"I know what we did." Hauk scrunches his nose. "Since when does Full-On Frakes concern himself with the right and wrong of things?"

"I never hurt anybody who didn't have it coming."

"That's a little squishy, but if it helps you sleep at night, I'll concede for the most part."

"It was wrong. Period." Frakes can barely get out the words. "Just wrong."

"Well, that's for the Lord to decide, I suppose."

"Bullshit." Frakes pushes Hauk off him, rushing to the other side of the room. Stands a few feet from Mama. "They had nothing to do with anything. You know it."

Mama tries to put a hand on him. "Son—"

"Don't. Please don't, Mama." Frakes pulls free. "Not the time."

"Remind me again when you sprouted a conscience." Hauk slow-stalks toward Frakes, wiggling his fingers with his faced balled into a question mark. "This is the game, man. Like I just told you, it gets damn messy from time to time."

Game?

Messy?

Frakes pounds his fist against the wall. He's losing what little control he has.

"What's done is done." Hauk tries to bring the temperature of the room down. "Can't put the toothpaste back. That genie is out the bottle."

Frakes can feel the gun tucked behind his back. Screaming at him, pleading to join the conversation. Wanting him to do what he knows has to be done. Blobs of white form at the edges of his vision. Teeth feel like they could grind to dust. Anger pulse needs to feed.

"We can only control how we react to life's bumps." Hauk looks to Tipton for confirmation.

Tipton nods fast. "Things happen."

"Listen to them, son," Mama pleads.

Bumps?

Things?

Frakes's vision narrows into a tunnel. A white, blinding, glowing outline around Hauk. Frakes eases his hand down by his side, positioned to make a move. He can have his gun pulled, finger on the trigger before this goes the wrong way.

"Last time I'm saying it. We did wrong, Hauk."

"Disappointed you feel that way."

Hauk slices Frakes's throat open.

"You do talk facts." Hauk looks into his fading eyes. "But it's gotta be the last time you say that shit."

Blood sticky and hot slips between Frakes's fingers before rolling out into a pour. A spray rips across Hauk's face. He rubs it into smears as he watches Frakes stumble back, hand stretched out reaching for Mama.

She steps back. Jaw dropped. A trembling hand over her open mouth.

Hauk cocks his head as Frakes falls to his knees, his free hand clawing at the wall. Tipton stands next to Hauk. Eyes dancing. Nibbling on his lip, terrified to speak.

Frakes yanks his gun out from behind his back. So weak he can barely hold it up, pointing, jamming it at things he can't even see. Full-on Frakes fighting while his last few ounces of life escape his hulking body.

Tipton ducks down. A bullet zips over his head, exploding a hole in the wall.

Hauk kicks Frakes's hand away, then stands on his wrist, pinning the gun to the floor. The ligaments crunch. Hauk presses his boot down harder, waiting for this to be over. Frakes struggles with what he has left, shifting his body, working to get his arm free from under Hauk's boot.

"You're a fighter." Hauk speaks soft and easy to his dying employee. "You've done some good work for me. That matters in this life. Matters big to me, at least." Frakes coughs. Blood strings into webs from his lips. "Hope you find some peace out there."

Frakes's fading thoughts are of the girl and boy.

He tried. He really tried to make it right the best he knew how.

He hopes they run far, far away, never to be found.

Frakes's body goes still. Heart barely pumping.

"Get up," Hauk barks at Tipton, who's face-down on the floor.

Hauk picks up the gun from Frakes's limp hand, slipping it into the front of his jeans. He pulls a dirty rag from his back pocket and wipes the blood from his face. Tipton pushes himself up off the floor, brushing off his uniform.

Hauk turns to Mama.

Her shaking hand fumbles for a smoke, her hand torch waiting in the other hand. The flame dances along with the rhythm of her trembling body.

"Easy there." Hauk's smile is wide and warm. "Allow me."

He places his hand on hers, gently pushing the cigarette to her mouth, then moves the flame to light the end. Mama nods a nervous thank you as tears roll down her cheeks.

"Better?"

Mama takes a long drag, then exhales a big cloud into the air above her.

"Yes."

"Fantastic."

Hauk pulls Frakes's gun, firing one bullet in her head. Her body wilts to the floor. Hauk watches her for a moment, waiting for the light to go out in her eyes.

"Do what you have to do. Whatever, but make it work," Hauk says to Tipton, tossing the gun near Frakes and then dropping his bloody knife at Mama's feet. "Make it look nice. Nobody will come out here for days. Good chance nobody finds them for a month. Get the word out that these two hated each other. Long history of family problems and so on. You get me?"

Tipton's mouth struggles to find a single word to say.

"Do you get me, sweetheart?" Hauk towers over him, sucking deep breaths in and out, waiting for an acknowledgement. "Let me hear that you hear me."

"I hear you, Hauk."

"Good. Don't fuck it up." Hauk storms away, not requiring more conversation.

The door slams behind him, adding punctuation to the moment. Tipton shudders as the house shakes around him. Windows rattle, then slow to a silent stop.

"I hear you," the broken whisper ekes out from his lips.

Tipton's feet turn him in tiny, nervous circles. Alone in a house surrounded by the staggering stillness that ripples after Hauk's violence. He knows Hauk will want more than just handling this house. He wants that New York, Wall Street guy and those kids. Like the song says—a shotgun needs an outcome—and Hauk will want results. Tipton rushes out the door. Needs to get to work. Now.

Frakes blinks.

Waiting to see the heels of Tipton's boots leave the room through his pinhole view.

Through his tunneling, failing vision, he watches the front door close.

What's left of his life will be counted in seconds.

His fingers fumble into his pocket. Slipping and digging, Frakes tries not to look toward Mama next to him. No time for grief or pity.

He slips his phone out from his pocket.

Fingers slip and slide on the glass, can barely make out what he's doing, but he taps out a text saying what needs to be said. Satisfied that he did one thing right. That he slipped that so-called *dumb phone* into the girl's pocket when Tipton showed up at the house. He was slick about it too. Cool like James Bond. Dropped it into her jacket pocket when he bumped into her. Makes him smile thinking about the move.

Stupid.

Stupid.

Stupid Eddie Frakes.

What's left of his sight is a mixture of globs and jagged rips of darkness. Consciousness is loose and light. All sound has left his ears. Feels nothing, weightless and weak. As the last of his blood spills, his fading thoughts are of the boy and girl.

They are running far, far away. Never looking back. Finding a life. A good one.

Hopes he somehow managed to tap Send on his final words to them. He wanted the kids to be together with her, maybe even tonight, but Frakes didn't know what to do. Everything slipped away from his control so fast. He just ran out of time.

Mama's gravel-and-gravy voice pours over his brain one last time.

Stupid.

Stupid.

Stupid Eddie Frakes.

"Shut up, Mama."

The anger pulse dulls, breaks, drifts away.

PART TWO

PART TWO

SEVENTEEN

NONE *of them had any idea what was coming.*

How could they?

There was no known threat on the horizon. No known enemies. No past darkness to summon harm to their picture-perfect life.

The girl and boy had only known love and kindness. Everyone they'd ever known—from their schools, their friends, their family, and so on—was all much like them. All going through life unaware someone savage could be lurking only an arm's length away.

The events of that night shattered everything they thought they knew.

Events that would send the boy and girl into the trunk of a stranger's car. Toss them into a metal shed in the woods. Eventually sending them running into those same woods in the middle of the day with nowhere to go and no one to go to.

It was cool that night, not cold, but nice.

The girl remembers that much, never asked her brother what he remembers. Not sure she wants to know. Not sure she wants to bring it up, risk unearthing or jarring loose any memories that might be buried under the surface of her brother's mind. Bad thoughts like worms wriggling in the dirt.

It's hard enough for her to think of the things she has twisting around in her head. She knows he's not as breakable as she makes him out to be, not like that vase Mom had that would crack if you sneezed too hard, but he's her little brother and she has to do whatever she can to protect him.

That's what sisters and brothers do, Mom and Dad always said. They may drive you nuts. You fight from time to time. But nobody on God's green earth should ever say an unkind thing about them, let alone mess a hair on their heads. Those words from her mom and dad ran through her mind every night in that shed.

She knows they helped her even if she can't explain how. She also knows that no matter what she does, she can't keep her brother from the memories of what happened. No way to fix that.

Mom and Dad are gone. That truth is cold, hard, and unthinkable, but still, it can't be argued.

They have each other and that's going to have to be enough.

The girl and boy were with their mom and dad that cool night. Sitting on the porch of the house they all loved eating popcorn, talking and laughing, sharing jokes and stories. She can still hear her dad's deep laugh. The sort of laugh he released when he really thought something was funny. Not that fake, being friendly laugh she heard him give sometimes at the store or at church.

They were going to sit down in the living room and watch a movie a little later. She and her brother fought about which movie. He wanted to watch some stupid superhero save-the-world blah-blah thing. She wanted to watch an animated movie. Not just some dumb cartoon, as her brother put it, but an animated movie with some heart and a message. Not to mention, she loved the songs, knew them by heart. Sure, there were talking animals but there was a point. A meaning. Something that required you to think even though it was beautifully animated fun.

A car pulled up to the house, headlights slicing through the night.

She remembers the dust settling in front of the

headlights, creating this weird look almost like smoke. As if the headlights were fiery eyes staring at them, able to cut through the dark with their power. Their mom and dad looked to one another. They weren't scared, not yet, but they also didn't look like they were expecting anyone either.

The car doors opened.

The girl didn't recognize any of the men who stepped out from the car.

At least not then. She and her brother would come to know one of them better than they wanted. One of them they'd come to know as the big, mean man. They'd go to the mean man's house and later meet his horrible mama. She remembers being afraid of him the second she saw him. Knew he was up to no good even while sitting on their porch.

Not sure she could point out any of the rest of the men with him, but one of them was even scarier than the mean man with the shed. She remembers he was big too, with a bald head that shined under the moon. He had tattoos that went all the way up to his face almost. Eyes like a demon, she remembers thinking. Doesn't remember seeing that police officer that night, but that doesn't mean he wasn't there.

The world got so scary so fast.

She could feel it in the pit of her stomach. Even now her insides twist like a pretzel just thinking about it. She can still smell the popcorn, hear their family's laughter hanging in the air as those men climbed out of the car. The men approached the house with things gripped in their hands. Some of those things were guns. One of them, the bald one maybe, had a baseball bat.

Their mom and dad stood up.

Dad said something about getting her and her brother inside.

The girl wasn't sure if he or Mom knew these men. Didn't look like they did. Maybe they did, but they were both so worried.

Mom tried to hide it from her and her brother, but she could see it as if she was holding up a sign. They were scared too, now that she really thinks about it.

Their mother moved them inside quickly. Dad looked back at them with what looked like a smile but it wasn't a real smile. Like those fake laughs, she knew the difference.

Never seen her mom or dad frightened by anything before.

Dad stayed on the porch, seemed like he was trying to be friendly with the men. His voice had a kindness to it. The men didn't say anything. They just had hard looks on their mean faces.

Mother moved her and her brother into the house and told them to go into the closet. Mom asked them to be quiet and stay down. Hide the best they could. Said Mommy and Daddy will take care of this. Her eyes were watery. She was shaking. May have been crying, but it kind of sounded like she was trying to convince herself that everything was going to be fine just as much as she was trying to convince them.

Everything happened so fast.

All her life, every day before that night, was bright and fun even if she hadn't realized it then. Part of her feels bad for ever complaining about anything before.

Those horrible things?

They happened faster than she could have possibly imagined. A blur of awful erasing every-thing she thought would last forever. Nightmares at three-times speed, like pressing fast-forward on the scariest part of the scariest movie she'd ever seen.

While she stayed awake in that mean man's shed, she'd replay it all, thinking how she could not believe how quickly everything went bad. In a snap. A light switch flipping from happy to sad.

Outside the closet, she heard voices rise.

Yelling and screaming.

Hard to tell who was who. There was a crack. Thumps and thuds. Then a loud boom, which she imagines was two quick gunshots and then one more. She'd never heard a gun before, but she was sure that's what it was. Then they heard her mother scream.

The girl covered her ears.

The boy sat wide-eyed. Stone-faced. As if he had been pulled out of cold storage. Kind of like he wasn't even there. He'd removed himself from what was happening somehow. Shutting down, willing himself to be anywhere but there.

The sounds got worse.

The worst of it she probably pushed away, shoved it out of her mind, but enough of it is still there. She knows there is more, so much more, but she tries not to think about it. Everything got louder and louder. The closet seemed to rattle and shake with the stomping footsteps.

There was a door slam.

Felt like a hurricane was tearing through the house. She was sure her heart was going to jump right out of her.

Then everything went quiet.

So quiet.

The silence was even more terrifying.

She remembers wishing that somebody would say something. Hoping there would be some kind of sound telling them it was over. Some kind of anything that would let them know everything was all right. She waited to hear Mom's and Dad's voices. For the door to open and see their smiling faces telling them that indeed everything was okay.

Seconds crawled like hours.

She couldn't take it anymore. She had to know. She called out, "Mommy!"

The boy pushed open the door and yelled even louder. In that moment, she held her breath, knowing right away that was a mistake. A big one. They were told to stay here and be quiet. They were told Mommy and Daddy would take care of everything.

Sounds of feet came stomping down the hall fast.

They didn't sound at all like Mom and Dad.

Why hadn't she listened to her mom?

What had they done?

She pulled her brother back into the closet and shut the door as quietly as she could. They held each other tight.

The closet door opened.

She knew then their lives would never be the same.

When that big, mean man opened the door, she knew their mom and dad were gone forever...

SHE FEELS a buzz in the pocket of her jacket.

She shakes her mind free from the claws of her memory. The sight of that big, mean man looking down at them as they huddled together on the floor of the closet. He had the same look each time he opened the metal door of the shed too. His head down. He wouldn't look at them. Shy or embarrassed or maybe even ashamed. It never made sense to her.

Her heart is racing at a hummingbird's pace.

Looking around, she realizes she must have drifted off. She and her brother are still on the cushy couch watching SpongeBob. They are safe, or what seems like safe for now, inside the humongous house with the maybe-nice-man called Hooper.

The buzz came from inside her jacket.

The dirty jacket that doesn't fit right. One that the big, mean man gave to her after pulling her and her brother out of the trunk that horrible night. About three sizes too big, but it helped with the cold nights some.

Another buzz from deep inside her pocket. One she never looked in or even thought to look in before. She knows what that buzz is. She's felt it before, but had no idea that it was in there now. The mean man gave her this phone one time. He said something about giving it to her so he could communicate with them when he needed to while they were in the shed.

In case of emergencies, he said.

She remembers throwing the phone back at the man's feet. She got scared when she saw it land in the dirt, not sure what he'd do after she did it. In that moment, she didn't care. She didn't want to communicate with him, on a phone or with anything else.

Now, she remembers maybe feeling something slip into the pocket of her jacket. It was when they were being pushed back into the house after that police officer showed up. It was all rushed, pushed along, but she felt the mean man nudge her toward the house, had no idea what was happening. It all happened so fast. No time to think about anything.

She reaches inside the pocket. Her small fingers feel the small phone, its cheap plastic running across her fingertips. Holding her breath, she removes the phone. The screen is lit up with the words of a new message.

Her breathing stops.

Hands shake.

Turning, she finds her brother still lost in the glow of SpongeBob on the massive screen. His mouth crunching away at his glorious Cheetos. She thinks of shaking him, getting his attention, but stops herself. Hooper stands just off the side of the couch. He's been walking back and forth for quite a while in the living room. Ever since his sister, Allison, left.

The girl looks to him. Hopes he'll see her.

Hooper is lost deep into his own head, doesn't notice her at first, but then he sees her staring at him. Her raised eyebrows, her little body bouncing on the cushion of the couch. Her unmistakable quivering lips begging to say something that he knows she won't let go of.

The girl raises the phone, extending her arm straight and showing him the screen.

Hooper comes around to her side of the couch, moves in close, his eyes squinting to read the tiny message on the glass screen. LED with black letters on a pale-yellow background. He stands back.

"Okay." He starts to say something more. Resets. "Do you know who that's from?"

The girl nods a yes. Lips tight together, blinking back the tears.

"Okay. Someone good or someone bad?"

He watches her small hands ball up into fists. Jaw tight like a vice. Hooper knows the answer before she forces out a word through clinched teeth.

"Bad."

Hooper nods, gently putting his hand out, asking if he can take the phone from her trembling hand. A look of relief washes over her. As if a great weight is being taken from her, she gently places the phone into his palm.

Hooper's heart falls.

So many questions about this phone, this message, and so much more. But he doesn't want to press her.

The girl's state is fragile and raw right now. Even the most incompetent of child caregivers can see that. He reads the screen again.

Not a long message, but the words land heavy and hard.

Ur mama still alive

EIGHTEEN

"YOU HEARD ANYTHING YET?"

Hooper holds the girl's small phone in one hand, his own gripped in the other. Needing some space to process, as well as a private place to talk to Allison, he stands in front of the sprawling window of the master bedroom upstairs.

A monument to natural, cool colors and over-priced charm. If you asked the coolest person on earth and your average grandmother to work together using only the most expensive stores to decorate a room, this would be it. An ivory white standalone bathtub with hand-carved lion's feet dug into the floor peeks out from the rolling door to the bathroom.

Hooper thinks of sliding into it, fully dressed,

and letting the water pour over him. But he doesn't. Instead, he stares out the glass letting the world pour its heavy weight down on him from head to toe. Can't help but feeling so small as he leans against the glass.

The enormity of the world outside the window screams, pointing out his insignificance. How petty and tiny he is compared to what's out there. How truly helpless we all are to whatever way the wind blows.

Someone misses a stop sign, killing a family of four.

A hurricane all but removes a city from the map.

A diagnosis for a condition that you can't wall off. One you can't talk or buy your way out of. So you create a fake psychopath in your mind —give him a cool yet fun name—to make it easier for your fragile mind to accept.

This situation, he thinks. *This impossible situation that's come knocking at my door.*

There's a buzz to his mind. An itch on his skin. The gnawing helplessness of not knowing how to help these children who came looking for help anywhere they could find it. And they have to settle for him. To be fair, he didn't ask for any of this. Not like he signed up to an email list or gave an extra two bucks at the register.

"But here we are," Hooper whispers to himself, waiting while Allison checks in with her sources. "Here the hell we are."

The window is like a wall-sized movie screen showing him looping scenes of the mountains and trees surrounding them. A real-life relaxation video sans the artificial white noise. A person could stand here for hours watching this little slice of the universe.

A different planet from where Hooper was only days ago. A city he thought was better than anything he'd ever seen before—New York. The home of all the best. The nightlife, the bars, the high-end restaurants that offered him the best table if he'd just ask for it, the publisher who kissed his ass. Of course, NYC was also the residence to all of his problems that he will never be able to escape.

Hooper knew a simple change of address wouldn't wipe the world clean for him, but he thought it might help clear the white board of gibberish scribbled across his jumbled mind.

True, it did erase it all for about five minutes.

More like two.

Now, there are all new lines being written

across his mind. And they ain't gibberish. These aren't ranting streams of nouns, verbs, and adjectives. His thoughts have a hard focus to them. Not to be too self-aggrandizing, but for the first time in a long time, perhaps forever, his thoughts aren't squarely about Hooper.

Sure, some of them are about him indirectly. Some directly as hell, if he's being honest, but the truth is he's thinking about these kids. There are questions being hurled at him too. Questions throwing quick jabs like surgical-strike punches.

What the hell happened to them?

What happened to their family?

Who is after them? Who sent this?

He reads the text again.

Ur mama still alive.

"Okay." Allison comes back to the call. "Think I've got some things to start with—"

"Think I've got something too." Hooper presses his forehead against the cool glass. "See if they can run something on a phone. The girl got a message from someone. Someone she knows, but ya know, she's not really a geyser of information."

These kids need help. That's been clear all along, but Hooper didn't realize how much or how badly they needed it until now. This is beyond taking a wrong turn in the woods or some pre-teen—or whatever they are—temper tantrum where they stormed away from home in a huff.

He, and now Allison, are the only ones who can help them.

The cops are a massive question mark. No one they know of to call on the kids' behalf. He wishes they would just talk to him. Wishes the kids would fill in some of the blanks here. One or two open spaces on the Hooper questionnaire would be insanely helpful.

A rush of cold pushes through his veins.

What if we hadn't stopped for pancakes?

What if I'd dropped them off at the police station?

Better to be lucky than smart. That was something their dad always told him and Allison. He always clarified that both is best, and the smarter you are about life the luckier you appear to be, but Hooper always just takes that first part and skips the details.

These fits of wisdom their father gave usually came during a board game or a drive to the store, but they always stuck with Hooper. He's tried to work his father's lines into as many books as possible.

Peeling his head off the window, he starts

tapping the dumb phone against his temple. As if this motion will magically send information into his skull. He can't believe how close he came to handing those kids over to the cops.

"She has a phone?" Allison asks. Hooper hears her turn signal clicking. She's turned down the music too. "That would have been useful information."

"I didn't know she had it. Not sure she knew she had it either. It's a cheap one. Not a flip thing but not far off."

The message seems to strongly suggest the kids thought their mother was dead. Probably killed. The girl's face went ghost white upon sight of the message. Hooper tried to ask her questions, but she couldn't even manage a nod or a shake of the head. Only a hint of a smile, an odd smile. Relief mixed in with all the terror, Hooper guesses.

Did that cop have something to do with their mother?

What about their dad?

"A burner?" Allison asks.

"No. I don't know, maybe, but it looks like one of those kid phones. Only calls one number. Also looks like someone did everything they could to make calling for help harder than hell."

"Got it." Allison takes a deep breath. "I can call Ross and Dutch back. Send me everything about the phone. The number, the number the text came from if you've got them. Take a picture of the front and back of the phone, see if it's got a SIM card inside, all that."

"Doing it now."

"Maybe they can do some sorcery with the cell towers and find the location the message came from. Should be enough for them to dig into at least."

Hooper taps speaker so he can talk while taking a picture of the back of the girl's phone, then texting it along with other details to Allison.

"Hey." Allison's voice cracks.

"Yeah?"

"What do you think is going on?"

"I don't know." Hooper looks to the stairs that lead down to the living room. Imagines those kids and all the horrible possibilities. "I wish they'd talk to me about some it. Any of it."

"Don't push them. You don't want them to shut down completely."

Hooper nods. He knows, but he needs to hear his sister work it through with him. If nothing else, to reassure him he's doing something correctly here.

"You've done good with them. You know that, right?"

"No. No I don't. This isn't my thing, Allison. You know that."

"I know that. The whole damn world knows that, but I also know you can do this."

"How the hell do you know that?" Hooper puts his head back on the window. "That sounds made up."

"Fine. Guilty." Allison fights through a laugh. "I sooo made that bullshit up. I don't know if you can do this. Hell, I don't even know what this is, but I know you. You're a mess. You're forty-eight percent asshole, but the rest of you is better than anyone I know. And if you can just yank your head from your ass for a minute and redirect that remaining fifty-two percent in a useful direction? Not much we can't do, big bad bro."

"Touching." Actually, he is touched but won't allow it.

"I'll call you back when I hear something."

Hooper taps the call away, tossing both phones onto the bed. As they bounce and then settle to a resting spot near a plush blanket, his mind rips through anything and everything.

The wife who said he'd be a horrible father.

His father. His father at his best moments. The things he said and how he said them.

Movie versions of perfect fathers, and those films about the worst fathers. The men he's written who were kind, strong, and good. The men he's thought about writing. The things they'd think, feel, and say. Hooper pulls all of them together, piecing together the best version of an imaginary man who would know what to do.

A fictional version of Hooper.

One who would know what to do and say.

His stomach slips into its now familiar knots. Ripples of nausea surface and the knots pull tighter and tighter. His phone buzzes on the bed. The meds app Allison installed on his phone is going off.

There's a pounding in his head.

Hard to parse what's his *condition* and what's the situation of his current houseguests. No reason to separate them, Hooper decides. They are one and the same in his mind now. One big blob of shit. Why bother separating?

Actually, now that he's digging into it, they are separate.

Of course they are, but there is an order to them. One needs to be dealt with long enough in order to solve the other. The meds will keep him upright and functional. Those kids need the best version of him, fictional or otherwise, not to mention functionally upright.

He had no idea what was coming when he decided to rent this place.

But those scared kids had no idea whose door they were knocking on. They were lost. Only knowing they needed to run away from whatever was chasing them. Those blended, smeared ideas of loss, hope, and fate have reached critical mass here. Maybe it's the perfect location, or it could be the oddest location ever. A collision here in this massive luxury home nestled in one of the most beautiful places Hooper has ever seen.

One thing cannot be avoided.

The four of them are in this together now. The girl and boy. Him and Allison. There's another certainty—whatever has happened to those kids has silenced them. They can speak, that much he knows. It's not a physical problem or a disability. It's clear they've made a choice not to speak.

There's a burning in the pit of his stomach. The idea that someone hurt or scared them so bad they won't even utter a full sentence. He has to find a way to get those kids to talk to him. Give him something. Anything.

"Time to get into character," he whispers to himself, adjusting his shirt.

Picking up both phones, Hooper heads down the stairs.

NINETEEN

Hooper takes a deep breath as his feet touch the living room floor.

No clue as to how he's going to do this.

Some ideas, but not good ones.

There's no playbook that he knows of. Maybe that one wife knew what she was talking about after all. Him and kids. Him being a disaster. He hasn't spoken to her in years, only seeing her name as an occasional line item when he talks to the money people. He sees more ex-wife-name line items than he'd care to mention, but he can hear her voice plain as day. Laughing out the sentence like a punch line.

You'd be a horrible father.

He knows all their names—the ex-wives—he just chooses to not think about them as what their parents called them. To be clear, he cared about all of them. That's the truth. At one time, he did feel what most would call love, perhaps lust mixed with affection, but some he truly cared deeply for. And if he's being honest, he still does care about them but thinking of them by name adds a personalized layer of pain to an already painful list.

A list of relationship failures that he's mostly responsible for. Sure, most failed marriages are the sum of two people not making it work for a variety of reasons. Even if one side is 99.9 percent to blame, the other side had some fault in it usually. Nobody comes out of life guilt free. Hooper, however, knows he holds a majority stake of the blame for each of his marital blunders.

So to spare himself any form of prolonged self-assessment, he chooses to not think of them as names and more as points they've made about him. Points he thinks might be valid. Things they've said about him that have teeth. The accuracy of them digging into him, leading to some half-assed moments of discovery.

Hooper's never been one for therapy, although he's self-medicated for years. He doesn't think it's for him. Not that he doesn't think therapy is useful. He's known people it's done wonders for, seen it help people be happy, or whatever passes for happiness.

Allison even set him up with a renowned therapist in Manhattan about a year ago. Dragged him to the appointments.

Hooper did then what he's about to do now.

He created a character, one who wasn't really him. Parts of him, as any character he's created is, but one who wasn't truly him. He manufactured a version of Hooper with a list of personal problems that weren't really his own. Solvable ones that he spoon-fed the therapist so it would seem like they made breakthroughs in the room.

He acted like a person who was open to therapy, served his time—the five sessions he agreed to when Allison begged him to go—and once those sessions were over, he wrote a book about a therapist whose psychotic patient was trying to kill him. It sold millions of copies worldwide. The eight-episode limited series won two Golden Globes and led to a three-project deal.

Hooper exhales.

He's come up with a character that just might work for talking with these kids. At this point, everything is like molding clay making progress toward a masterpiece, but he thinks he's got some good bones to a fictional someone who might say the right things here.

This version of Hooper is a single father with a quick wit whose love is sometimes masked behind his sarcasm but also one who knows he needs to open his heart to his kids.

He's scared that he's losing them.

The custody battle has been hard on everyone. The children have become distant, walled off since their mother left with that douchebag periodontist—this actually happened with one of Hooper's wives; helps when he sprinkles in some real-world examples—and this single father of two just wants to connect with his son and daughter before he loses them forever.

It feels a little melodrama, he knows.

Maybe too much bad '90s TV show vibe, but it's what Hooper's come up with on the fly. Regardless of how he gets there mentally, he needs those kids to talk to him. No matter the mask he slips on, this is the only way Hooper knows how to help them. And if this bullshit *didn't get renewed for a second season TV single father bit* gets him there, then so be it.

As he slips out of his own head and into character, he can hear a cartoon voice.

Ever dopey but always charming.

Scanning the living room, the TV still burns bright but the channel has moved onto another cartoon. One he doesn't recognize. The girl and boy aren't there. Only an empty couch.

Hooper's heart skips a row of beats.

"Hello?" he asks the room.

Turning to the kitchen, he hopes to see that they went searching for more Cheetos.

Empty.

The entire first floor of the house feels small, gutted. Only minutes ago, it seemed vast. A space that was almost too open with too much space to feel comfortable in. Now the air feels tight. The walls getting closer and closer.

He checks the hallway.

Empty.

"Hey," Hooper calls out. Coughs. Words getting caught in his throat. "You kids here?"

Nothing.

"Hiding or some silly shit?"

Booming silence.

Hooper walks quickly down the hall, steps turning into a jog as his mind is already flipping through mental pages of all the horrible things that might be happening.

Who sent that text?

The cop at the diner?

What happened to their parents?

Spinning into the game room, he finds nothing. Only the glasses from when he talked with Allison sit empty on the bar. Pushing himself off the doorframe, he runs hard down the hall toward the back of the house. Stopping, skidding in quick jerks, looking into the smaller rooms one after the other.

Each one dark and empty.

"Hello?" he calls out. "Not funny. Come on out, please."

At the end of the corridor is a large picture window with a view of the front part of the house. A bird soars, slicing up the blue sky into two halves like a flying blade. To his left is a door that he thinks maybe leads to a deck of some kind. No, wait. Ronnie said there's a storage area in there. An axe for Manhattan hipster douchebags.

There's a panel near the door. Looks to be a screen for the security system. One he vaguely remembers the superstar real estate agent saying something about. Saying there are cameras and sensors with timed lights.

Really wishes he'd listened to her more.

Maybe Ronnie knows how all that works.

There's a tiny sneeze at the far end of the

corridor. He turns, spinning around so fast he loses his footing. Stumbling down, he presses off the floor with his palm. His feet pound the hardwood floors racing toward another room that almost seems to have an unnatural glow to it from so much natural light pouring in.

Jerking to a stop, he's reached what looks like a library of sorts.

Bookcases that reach to the ceiling. All polished, deep, rich cherry wood with one of those iron ladders that runs along a track so someone can reach the books at the top.

Walls of glass beam sunlight over Hooper's shoulder as he fights to catch his breath. His heart is in his throat but relief is working its way through him.

The boy is playing on the ladder, treating the library like a playground at a fast-food joint. The girl sits staring out the window. She's never looked so tiny to Hooper. She's swallowed up by the chair like a lost child in a fairy tale hiding in a castle while the creatures of the dark forest lurk.

Hooper assumes she didn't tell the boy anything about the text given how much fun he is having with the ladder. Maybe that's the thought she's considering so hard. Looks to be turning it over and over in her mind. Walking through the steps of telling him while twisting the ends of her hair so tight the tip of her finger is growing purple.

"Okay." A chop of a word comes through his sharp breaths. Hands planted on his knees. "Good. You found the books. Reading's good."

Hates himself for wanting to check if any of his books are here. His eyes have already started scanning the rows for familiar covers. Color patterns. He stops himself. Does his ego-fueled bullshit have no bounds? He already knows the unfortunate answer.

"I need you to talk to me."

The girl and boy turn to him.

It just came out.

Hooper's mouth threw the syllables out into the world without a bit of shine. Surprised even himself.

Not the line his carefully curated '90s single dad character would have said at all. Out-of-character dialogue. Too on the nose. Something buried deep in Hooper's mind short-circuited all that. Clarity is needed here.

Maybe it was while he was running down the hall scared for what might have happened to them. Perhaps it's the look on the girl's face that stopped his master plan before it began.

His guts twist. He can't believe it. Anger grows, angry at himself for not realizing the most obvious connection between him and these children.

Idiot, he thinks.

He's a grown man and he still can't process the deaths of his father and mother. So very different than anything these kids have experienced, but it still lands in a similar way. The deaths of his parents hit him in a specific yet undefinable place. One he has walled off to visitors.

Hooper gets lost in her glazed stare.

She's a child.

Younger than he was when his father passed, and Hooper can only guess that whatever is going on with these kids isn't the same. No kind nurses or doctors calmly explaining things. No private, quiet rooms to sit in. No family and friends attempting to be of comfort to them. Not one single person is asking to help them.

It hits him like a falling rock.

Eyes water. Deep breath sucked in. Slow breath pushed out.

"Look. Let's cut the shit. Can we cut the shit?" Hooper clears his throat, motioning for the boy to come over and take a seat next to his sister.

The boy can't help but giggle off *shit*.

It appears to have landed with the girl as well. Eyes brighten up a little.

"I can't help you if you don't talk to me." He keeps his distance but takes a small step closer. "I'm here. Not leaving you. And to be clear, I do want to help. Okay?"

The girl and boy do nothing at first.

They both lower their heads, refusing to look his way, but they do eventually give a nod. Hooper exhales. Didn't even know he was holding his breath.

"And Allison?" the boy says.

"Unbelievable." He shakes his head in disgust. "Yes, she wants to help too."

The boy looks to his sister. The girl turns, going back to staring out the window, watching the trees sway gently in breeze. She's maybe blinked once since Hooper came flying into the room.

"Something has happened to you. You don't have to tell me everything. Not even close. But I do need to know a little bit."

Hooper wipes away the tiny beads of sweat from under his skull cap. Or is it a beanie? Skull cap is cooler but he struggles with the correct name. There's a level of heat that has spiked since he's entered the room. Rubbing his hair that's been cut close to his skull, he counts backward, feeling the furnace his body has become. With each passing digit his temperature comes down.

Another little trick the doctor showed him, or maybe it was Allison. His fingers press ever so slightly, feeling the notches and divots along his head that he never knew were there before his new unwelcomed look.

The girl steals a glance his way, scrunches her nose, then turns back to the window before the nice man sees her looking at him.

Hooper slips the knit skull cap back on. He hates wearing it, but still isn't comfortable enough yet to not have it on all the time. Used to love his hair.

As his shoulders come down, he feels the phone shift inside his pocket. The girl's. The one with the text he so much wants to ask about.

Kills him not to say something, but he doesn't want to blow up anything the girl is doing. If she hasn't told the boy anything about the text, then Hooper certainly doesn't want to be the one to tell him. To suggest things are fragile right now is the understatement of the century. She's managing that situation. She has the ball.

Still, Hooper came racing into this room for a reason.

He thinks of the character he created. Maybe that guy knows what to do here.

Do better, he hears Allison's voice rattle inside his head.

Hooper takes a seat next to them, removes his beanie and holds it tight in his hands, tells the '90s single dad that his role has been cut and to please go home.

"You're safe here." Hooper feels his voice crack. Wasn't counting on the surge of emotions. "Whatever *safe* means right now. But I can't keep you safe unless you talk to me."

The boy locks into Hooper's eyes, nodding along as he speaks.

This is the first true connection between him and the boy. He has avoided Hooper for the most part, only looking to his sister for guidance. Maybe it's his deep puppy love for Allison, but it doesn't matter, Hooper will take what he can get right now. The boy taps the girl's shoulder. She ignores him.

"Can I start with one question? It's an easy one, I promise."

The boy nudges her, then again harder, almost pushing her onto the floor. The girl grips the fat arm of the chair, then shoves her brother back with everything she has.

The boy presses his lips tight together, eyes wide as pies, then pushes his head toward Hooper. A clear *talk to him* signal if ever there was one.

The girl's face twists into a mix of annoyance and more annoyance.

Hooper recognizes the look of a sister who's had it with her damn brother but can't ignore his bullshit forever. The girl and boy share a silent sparring match for what seems like forever. The seconds pound away at Hooper like heavyweight punches. Her face races through shades of red. The girl's frustration is reaching maximum—

"Ask it."

Her voice is way too hard for her age.

Hooper barely gets out the word *what*, stopping just short of cowering in a corner away from the girl's searing eyes.

"Ask your easy question."

Hooper does a quick calculation. That's a four-word response he just got from the girl. The longest conversation he's had yet. That's progress no matter how you slice it. Hooper knows this is the moment he needs to nail. He's got one shot at this.

"Please," her brother adds.

Holy shit.

There's a tiny crack opened up, shields dropped and they will either slam it shut or maybe, just maybe, open it a little more.

"Okay." Hooper resets. Clears his throat once more. "Do you guys like anything other than Cheetos?" He pulls his credit card, angling the platinum in the sunlight. "I'm buying."

The girl and boy smile the most amazing smiles Hooper has ever seen.

TWENTY

HOOPER WALKS the aisles of the small-town grocery store.

It wasn't a long drive in, but it was gorgeous.

The store is only a couple of blocks away from the diner. He fought all of his instincts to stop in and grab a cup of that delightful coffee, but decided he was on a bit of a clock with the children. He'd left them alone in that massive house.

Torn by what to do, he finally settled on the idea they were better off there rather than coming with him based on the morning run-in with that cop. Not that leaving them alone with that massive house was an easy choice. He knows he won't be gone too long, but still.

He told them to stay in the game room with

the TV. The room only has the one window and Hooper closed the blinds before he left. Thought about setting the alarm, but of course he'd have to know how it works in order to do that.

Reviewing his phone, scanning the shelves, he works through the list moving up and down the aisles of the small-town store.

Can't remember the last time he did any shopping like this. Usually has everything delivered, or he'll hit up a bodega for small items while roaming the city. This is kind of nice, he thinks, checking an unknown local brand. There's a peace to walking, looking around, letting life be absorbed by an instrumental version of "Paradise City."

Hooper had tapped out diligent notes.

Actually, he transcribed the series of one-word descriptions the girl wrote down for each item they requested. She found a fancy pen and paper in the library. The boy stopped her on some items on the list, shaking his head no in disagreement while looking over her shoulder. He'd whisper into her ear, she'd bite back her annoyance the best she could, either agreeing with his assessment or throwing out a hard veto, standing firm on her original order.

The list is standard kid fare. A nutrition-less

buffet of corporate taste-bud manipulations designed to enslave and/or kill us all. Hooper gets off his high horse, realizing that he's lived off bourbon and anabolic-enhanced steak for the last ten years. But he jogs, dammit. Does some yoga and throws in the occasional salad. That must count for something in this life.

He tosses three boxes of mac and cheese into the cart. The good stuff, not that no-name crap. Hooper remembers the days of shopping with his mother after his dad died.

Coupons, two for one, almost expired meat. A jolt of shame hits him for being such a snob about the mac and cheese. The joys of chemically enhanced pasta coated in cheese—no matter a person's level of income—isn't lost on best-selling author Nicholas Hooper.

As the last box peels from his fingers, his sight tilts.

The world shifts.

As if the floor took a hard, fast lean to the right. Hooper steadies himself, gripping the cart tight. The shopping aisle has narrowed, shrinking into a thin tunnel.

A flash of light, then spots of black. Only for a moment, then it's over. He's able to blink it all away, the tunnel vanishes, his view of the world is now level, but even Hooper can't deny what just happened to him.

His hand vibrates.

Looking to his buzzing phone, the app Allison installed has popped up a line of notifications from the top of the screen rolling down to the bottom.

Shit.

He didn't take his meds before he left the house.

His mind was somewhere else. Distracted by the fear that the kids weren't in the house. He was racing through the halls, then the mini breakthrough with them in the library. It's a complete cop-out to blame those kids for skipping his meds —there's no doubt he'd rather eat his arm than take the pills—but it's better than no excuse at all.

He struggles to find some moisture in his mouth. It's simply not there.

A desert of teeth and tongue. In his mind, he sees the meds perfectly sectioned off in their self-contained homes, sitting, waiting for him on the kitchen island. Not unlike an umbrella you left in the car during a storm thinking, *oh it won't rain, what do they know?*

Hooper tries to calculate how many doses he's missed.

When did I last take the pills?

They said there might be days like this. The body adjusting and so on.

What do they know?

His knees wobble. Legs feel like Jell-O. The world tilts again, only even harder this time. A now glowing tunnel takes up his vision.

"You okay, Mr. Hooper?"

Turning his head, he drops down to one knee. Recognizes the voice. In the center of the glow, Ronald stares back at him.

His own personal Ronnie.

Hooper's mouth forms a loose smile like he's on the wrong side of a five-day drunk.

"Hey, man." Not even sure what came out of his mouth. "Not okay at all."

The glow closes, swallowed up in black. Hooper feels his body melt away.

The store's tile is hard and cool. Glad he can still feel anything. Hands grab his shoulders. He hears Ronnie's voice but can't tell what he's saying. Muted tones with hints of concern.

"Get me to the house." Doesn't even sound like his own voice. "I have to help those kids."

TWENTY-ONE

SHE TOLD her brother about the message.

The text from the big, mean man.

Told him that it said that Mommy was still alive. He didn't say anything, still too broken to speak.

She gets it. Understands. She's not ready yet to be as chatty as she was before either. Not like she was before that night in the closet, but something has shifted inside her today.

Maybe it's the maybe-a-nice-man.

Maybe it's the hope the mean man is telling the truth and Mommy is still out there.

She doesn't know and doesn't care about who's mean and who's nice at the moment. What she cares about is her brother and finding their mother.

While her brother didn't say anything about the text message, he did cry. Cried hard. Harder than she's ever seen. The tears are still fresh on his cheeks.

She tells him she thinks they can trust this other man. This Hooper. He seems nice. Her brother just looked at her, not sure if he's thinking the same thing. She knows her brother likes the woman, Hooper's sister Allison, but that has nothing to do with safety. He just thinks she's pretty.

Sucker for a pretty face, their daddy used to say about him.

She squeezes her eyes tight just thinking about Daddy. Deep down inside, she knows those men killed him. In a nightmare, she heard the sound of it again. Never sure if it was her brain making it up or if it was an actual memory.

Tells herself to focus on the positive. That's what Daddy would have said. What he'd want them both to do.

"Focus on the positive," she says. "Okay?"

Her brother's head jerks up. Sobbing stops. He knows where those words came from.

"We have a roof over our head. Food. Water." She's echoing a tone and style their father would have used if he was sitting there with them. He'd given them both this exact speech several times before. "We can overcome anything if we stick together."

He nods. He silently mouthed the words *food* and *water* along with her.

"Maybe Hooper can help us find Mommy."

He scrunches his nose. Not so sure about that last one.

"I think he can. I think he's okay."

He offers her a half-hearted nod. She will take what she can get.

There's a noise at the front door. She reaches under the couch, pulling out the butcher knife she's moved from place to place with her. Always making sure Hooper never saw her doing it.

Trust but verify was also something Daddy always said.

She grips the large knife in her tiny hand. The blade almost as big as her head.

Someone has opened the front door. They can hear it from here. Her brother's eyes pop wide, his breathing heavy. She places a finger to her lips, letting him know what they both already know. Silence is golden.

"Hello?" a voice calls out from the living room.

A woman's voice. One they both know. The boy perks up.

The door opens and Allison steps into the room. She takes note of the girl's knife, putting her hands up. The girl lowers the blade, putting it back under the couch.

"Hi, Allison," the boy says.

The girl rolls her eyes.

"Hi," Allison says, setting down her overnight bag. "I see everything's somewhat okay here."

The boy and girl nod with a shrug.

"Soooo." She clucks her tongue. "My brother around?"

TWENTY-TWO

"Take it to the Limit" plays.

The live version.

Hooper fades in and out, soft-singing words while riding shotgun in Ronnie's rusted red truck. Forgotten how much he loves the Eagles. Reminds him of being drunk in high school, which is kind of how he feels right this second.

This Ronnie, he's all right.

The local hospital *fixed him right up*. Their words. Luckily, Hooper was lucid enough to tell them about his condition and showed them his various apps that had all his medical blah-blah coded in their digital, cloud storage mega-brains.

After passing out in the grocery, he remembers the feeling of hands moving, sliding, and picking him up. Muted, muffled voices close by but sounding so far away at the same time. Next thing he knew he was laid out in a hospital bed with more people pushing and poking at him. Tubes and needles. Rushes of cold and warmth.

They shined lights.

Asked him questions.

He muttered some things here and there. They seemed to understand, then he somehow managed to unlock his phone and pull up one of the apps. The nurse looked it all over while nodding away, telling the doctor a variety of terms Hooper's sure he's heard before but couldn't tell you what they were. *We'll fix you right up*, the doc said. Hooper vaguely recalls a lecture about taking his meds on time.

"You okay over there, buddy?" Ronnie asks, turning down the music.

Hooper gives a thumbs-up, reaching over and turning it back up. "Desperado" is coming up next, dammit. Placing his face back on the passenger window, the cool glass is like a wall of mild ice soothing his rattled psyche. Reminds him of when he was in the master bedroom only a few hours ago staring out into the woods, forming the backstory of his character that fell apart so quickly.

Might need some rewrites.

This is the first time he's had anything like this happen to him. His body shut down. It gave up without much of a warning either. There's that fear balling up in his stomach again. One born from understanding what little control he has. There's more to it, however. Hooper saw those kids' faces flash across his mind as he fell to the grocery floor.

What if that happened when I was with them?

If that happened when they needed me the most?

The pang of his celebrity hits him. Hopes there wasn't a wave of bullshit fired off about him being in the hospital. He had the same concerns about going to the police, but that was a lifetime ago. This time his concern isn't the damage to his author brand.

This time the concern is someone will use that information to find him. He can't connect all the dots right now, his head is a mess, but it stabs fear into his heart.

Did the cop see the kids?

Hopes a nurse or patient didn't recognize him. Hell, they had his books in that small store in the lobby. Even in his fragile state he saw the covers as they wheeled him in. Has to admit it was nice to see even in his damaged state.

Privacy means nothing anymore.

There are no boundaries, and if somebody recognized and thought it would make them look cool for five seconds, they'd post something anywhere and everywhere. And if that happened, then there's a chance the wrong people could see it—like that cop from the diner that Hooper's young guests were terrified of—and then come to find them.

"Ronnie?" Hooper smacks his lips.

"Yeah?"

"Did anyone say anything about me?"

"They said a lot about you. You were sort of the star of the show. Said you should take your medication. Said you're lucky this wasn't much worse. Said—"

"No. Did anyone say anything about me being an author or anything like that?"

"You write?"

Hooper smiles.

Before today, that little exchange might have caused a small ego-explosion within him. The idea that not everybody, not even one single person, recognized him as a best-selling author would ignite a bonfire of self-hate. Might have steered him straight to the bottle or started another doomed marriage just to make things feel okay for him. Fill up the pit that could never, ever be considered full.

Is this progress?

Or is it the drugs?

Either way, Hooper will take the win. As they round the turn making their way up the grass-dirt driveway, he sees his sister's car. He breathes a sigh of relief. There's no one he'd rather see right now.

That would go to her head, so he must never let her know that.

Ever.

TWENTY-THREE

HAUK WAS eight when Daddy left.

Ten when his mom died.

She was killed by her latest boyfriend while Hauk lay on the floor in the next room. He knew where his mom hid the gun in the house. She thought he didn't, if she ever thought about it at all, but Hauk knew she kept it in a shoebox in the hall closet of the dilapidated apartment they lived in.

He always thought it was a dumb place to put the gun, considering she spent most of her time on earth in that bedroom. So much time with what seemed like an endless supply of men. They stank of booze and smoke. Ragged, rough men of all shapes and sizes, until one decided she didn't need to breathe anymore.

Regardless, Hauk wiped the tears from his eyes, pulled the gun from the box in the hall closet and shot her last boyfriend three times. He still remembers the sound of the body when it twisted and then dropped to the floor. Like a 220-pound bag of shit dropped by God.

Hauk spent twenty-plus years of life in and out of various state facilities. Checking in and checking out like a long-term motel guest. So many programs designed to help him. And they did. Hauk was able to pull together a useful skill set for himself. Not in woodworking or metal works. He didn't study law or find the Lord.

Hauk knew he was smart, or smart enough— his daddy taught science and shit at a local high school before he got caught touching girls he shouldn't be touching—and Hauk knew how to manipulate and intimidate people. To him it was like breathing.

So while he was bouncing around from place to place, house to house, street to street during his formative years he honed these skills. Set his mind right.

An old-timer told him once to strike first, strike hard and fast.

Hauk took this to heart. He's cut and carved his way through what they call the criminal underbelly that lives and breathes right next to the *good people* of the world. He's made and lost so much money selling drugs and whatever else to those fine folks of the morally correct society he hears so much about.

Folks who are good until they want to be bad, but only long enough to scratch that itch of sin and then go back to their lives of cushy jobs, vacation time, and endless streaming entertainment. Doesn't bother Hauk, quite the opposite. He's glad those uppity pieces of shit are out there. It's what keeps him going.

People within Hauk's little organization—a staff that's constantly in flux—wonder why he still lives in an old, two-story house out in the middle of nowhere.

It's not bad, at least in Hauk's eyes. Needs some work, sure, a lot of work if anyone was brave enough to say it, but it's certainly not the home you'd think a criminal overlord would inhabit. Tony Montana's mansion it is not.

People come and go out of this five-bedroom place. Guns always present. Sounds of video games, '80s metal, and rough, yet casual sex echo throughout the halls no matter the time of day. Drugs are distributed and funds collected from a certain room that is off-limits to most of Hauk's guests.

Hauk calls that room Fort Knox.

Calls his room the Lion's Den.

Hauk sits in the Lion's Den on the edge of his bed. His leg bounces. Teeth grind. He needs his time. Been stressful since he found out about Frakes and those kids.

A baggie filled with pink-white powder rests on his bouncing leg. His eyes are zeroed in on the baggie. He looks away—a spike of disgust—then looks back. Slow and careful, he reaches behind him for his gear.

A master bedroom by definition, but it serves as a sanctuary of sorts of Hauk. He keeps stacks and stacks of DVDs and CDs along the walls. Thinks the quality is superior, but he also doesn't like the idea of digital footprints. Never uses email or cell phones. Hell, he still has one of his people bring him a daily paper brought from a store in town. Always pays in cash too.

Hauk's known far too many good people who have gone down in that ocean. Letting the convenience of the modern world compile evidence on you. Allowing the world, not to mention the law, to know where you are and what you're doing all the damn time. No thank you, sir. For Hauk, technology maxed out in 1995.

Visitors to the house must drop their devices off in a metal bin on the hill. A spot that's about a mile off the front gate to this place. Hauk's set up checkpoints. Lookouts, not cameras. All this managed by fear.

Every once in a while, someone will bring a date—boy or girl—into the house and Hauk will catch them doing a goddamn selfie or some shit. Hauk loves those moments. Teaching moments he likes to think of them as.

Hauk uncurls the twisty from the baggie. Holds it with his teeth. He taps out a little crank. That's what he still calls it, sure the dipshit kids have a cooler name. He doesn't give a shit about the ever-changing names of things.

A nugget drops down onto his favorite mirror.

When those teaching moments present themselves, he will beat that boy or girl within an inch of their lives, making a big production of it too. Makes sure everyone sees it. Then he'll set them up with a doctor and hand them some cash.

It's the power of sudden violence followed by just-as-sudden kindness that keeps his people together for the most part. He learned that technique from a pimp a while back. Decided to apply it to more broad situations. Outside-the-box thinking, he once heard someone say.

Then there's other people who just have to go away. A beating with a chaser of kindness sadly won't do the job sometimes. Those folks must go all the way gone.

Balancing the mirror on his thigh, he smashes the nugget into powder and divides it up into thin lines. Pulls out a red-and-white striped straw, taking a moment to collect his thoughts.

Savor the moment. The calm before.

Hauk sucks all that ephedrine, ether, and anhydrous ammonia up his nose. Snorts hard. Sits upright. Pinches his nostrils tight.

His mind travels. Random and euphoric.

Free, meandering, untethered by the here and now. Like animals in a children's cartoon. There's singing colors. Dancing shapes. He thinks of that house. That closet. The one Frakes was told to make the problems inside of go away.

"All the way gone," Hauk whispers through a fading smile, standing up from the bed lost in the swirling universe of his mind.

Time has zero meaning when he's like this. He'll stay in here for hours and hours until something or someone brings him out of it. Likes to choose moments when his calendar is mostly cleared. He curls his toes into the carpet as if holding on.

There's a soft knock at the door.

Hauk turns on the balls of his feet, eyes bulging, staring at the door as if willing whoever is there to come in or fuck off. Slips his finger on the trigger of his gun, keeping it at his side.

"Hauk?" Tipton says.

His voice is respectful. It better be.

"Come on," Hauk barks.

Tipton enters the room. The second he lays eyes on Hauk, he knows this was a bad time to stop by.

"I've got something," he says, clearing his throat, keeping his distance.

"Do you?" Hauk rubs his temple with the barrel of his gun.

"That guy. The one from the diner... I can come back later."

"Yeah, go on."

"Think I got something on him."

"Okay." Hauk circles the gun in the air, annoyed with Tipton. "You charge by the hour? Tell me what the hell you have."

"His name is Nicholas Hooper. He writes books." Tipton puts a cigarette in his mouth, looking to Hauk to see if it's okay if he smokes. Hauk waves on the smoke.

"An author?"

"Yeah, that."

"What kind of stories does the man write?"

Tipton shrugs out an *I don't know*.

Hauk shakes his head. Genius detective, this one.

"This writer, author, Hooper, he fell apart at the grocery. Some medical something. The ambulance got him, that's how my office got called. They fixed him up or whatever, but Ronnie is the one who was with him."

"I know Ronnie. Good man."

"Yeah, Ronnie is all right, but he does maintenance or whatever on those houses. The only way this Hooper guy would know Ronnie is if—"

"He's renting one of those houses."

"Yes, sir." Tipton snaps his fingers. "I didn't want to go digging around too much. Leave a trail of us looking into this guy."

"No. No. You did good, Officer Tipton."

Tipton takes a step back. He's held his tongue on this point for a while and has never said anything before. He's worked hard to become a cop and working with Hauk helps keep the peace regardless of how some people might see it. Maybe now, in this state, is the perfect time. Maybe not, but Tipton has to say something.

"Hauk. I know you're being funny, but I really don't like it when you call me *Officer*. It's the way you say it. There's this tone—"

The second it leaves his mouth he knows he may have made the biggest mistake of his life.

The muscles in Tipton's body go tight, as if he just tossed his lit cigarette under a gas can.

Hauk cocks his head birdlike.

"Sorry." Tipton backtracks. Words spitting out like bullets. "You're just messing around. My head, it's a disaster. Been on this all night. I didn't mean shit by what I just said. I'm too tired—"

Hauk shushes him like a child. Smiles. Motions for him to continue talking as he creeps closer to him.

"Anyway. Nobody has touched the Frakes house yet." Tipton backs up. Jumps off the feel of the wall behind him. "I'm on it. Keeping that all quiet for you."

"Good." Hauk's inches away from Tipton. "Great to hear."

"You..." Cold seeps deep into Tipton's bones. "You think those kids are at one of those houses, Hauk? This Hooper guy is hiding them?"

"Well, Officer Tipton." Hauk wipes the barrel of his gun across Tipton's lips like a tube of lipstick. Pauses, bounces his eyebrows, then forces the cold metal into Tipton's mouth. "Let's give all that a good, solid little think."

Tipton turns his head away like child who won't take his medicine.

Hauk wraps his thick fingers around his jaw, pushing down hard. Jams the gun between Tipton's teeth. Shoves the gun toward the back of the tongue until the knuckle of his trigger finger presses Tipton's quivering lip. Hauk nods, pleased as punch as his boy chokes and gags, spitting sprays along the sides of the barrel.

"This Hooper fella? What house you think he's got those littles in?"

Tipton gags hard, shaking his head side to side.

"Oh. You don't know?" His eyes are wild and wide, crank working miracles in management. "Well, officer. We are going to figure all that the fuck out. Aren't we?"

TWENTY-FOUR

RONNIE GIVES Hooper a hand stepping down from his truck.

It's a big, potentially ankle-breaking, tumbling gap between Hooper's reaching feet and the ground. He's still getting his legs back and might not be able to stick the landing. Feels good to have his head cleared up somewhat at least, but the rest of his body is still catching up.

Hooper imagines this being what old age is like. For some, the mind still has some flight left to it while the body is stuck on the ground, left behind. For others, there's neither. Hooper would rather not dwell on either version of potential old age too much.

Then it hits him.

A dark *duh* moment he can't believe he's

having.

None of that will be an issue for him. Old age won't be a thing for him.

Is that a positive? Never really considered it. Sure, thoughts of his demise have been lighting up his synapses recently, but this is the first time he's felt his death as an approaching thing. The notion of it being near. Creeping, crawling closer to him with each exhale from his lungs. Every thump of his heart ticking away precious time.

A flood of fears rises, filling up inside.

His vision blurs into a distant trance. Different from when he was at the grocery. This feels more like he's peeling away, drifting off from the planet. No character on the call sheet to bring in for this scene.

Then, as if on cue, hitting the mark with craftsman-like precision, his finely tuned self-defense measures push back the fear. Shoving it somewhere new, even deeper inside of him. A deep, dark place beyond where he locks the everyday, everything items he'd rather avoid. This is a special spot, even though he knows it'll find a way out. Chewing away at the ropes until it's free. At least maybe Hooper will make it into the house before that happens.

"Now, you take your pills when you get in

there," Ronnie says, balancing Hooper on a wall near the door. "Doctor's orders."

Hooper shakes loose from his trance.

"Yeah, yeah." Hooper fumbles to find the key to the door, patting himself down. "I'm a big boy."

Stuffs his hands down into his pockets searching. He put the house keys on that Chewbacca chain Allison gave him. Recalls slipping them on the ring right after the superstar real estate agent handed them over so they'd hang with his car keys, less chance he'd lose them. What the hell did he do with those damn—

There's a soft jingle.

Ronnie holds the keys out by the top of Chewbacca's head.

As Ronnie places them into his waiting palm, Hooper nods in defeat, acknowledging his *big boy* status is in serious question. Mouths a *thank you.*

Ronnie shrugs, turning and walking back to his truck. An unexpected slap of sadness hits Hooper. A wanting to keep his buddy here a little bit more.

"That it?" Hooper stands up straight, testing his balance. "You taking off? Leaving me with my sister? She's mean, you know."

"So you said." Ronnie lowers the tailgate, releasing a big creak of steel. He picks up a large, faded blue cooler by the handles, removing it from the bed of the truck. Looks like the cooler has had quite a life.

"Think I got all of it." Ronnie sets the cooler down at Hooper's feet. Opens it up.

Inside are bags of groceries.

Hooper shakes his head in quiet disbelief. Most of the items in the cooler are the things Hooper had in his cart. That is, before he dropped to the floor. But there's a few here he knows he didn't get the chance to pick out. Hooper realizes he had a list sitting in the cart. The items the girl scribbled down—in consultation with the boy—on a piece of that fancy stationery that was in the library.

Seems like an entire lifetime ago, but Hooper remembers her sweet, sometimes breaking, voice list the things they wanted. Random things from the store that Hooper guesses would give her and her brother comfort.

Hooper stares, mind still fuzzy around edges while processing, then looks up to Ronnie. This guy Ronnie, he pretty much saved his life, then finished shopping too.

It's probably a mix of the drugs and his fragile, emotional state of mind, but Hopper can't stop himself from hugging Ronnie tighter than he's ever hugged anyone before. Not sure he's ever initiated a hug in his life. Certainly not one with a man he's known for maybe less than an hour collectively.

"Yeah, yeah." Ronnie pats him on the back. "You'd have done the same."

"Doubtful." Hopper steps back, wiping the corners of his eyes. No crying, man.

"You take care of those kids, Hopper."

Hopper stops. "What?"

"Those kids who showed up at your door," Ronnie says, walking back to his truck. "You won't need me to help them now that you're upright. Besides, your *mean as shit* sister is here—your words, not mine—though she sounds like she's pretty all right from what you've said."

Hopper stares back at him. Blinks. No memory of this conversation at all.

"When you were on the floor at the store you told me a little bit about it all. The kids. Your sister. Said if you don't make it, for me to take care of them." Ronnie shuts the truck door. "I'm a nice guy but I ain't Santa Claus, and ya know, you've clearly made it, so here we are." Smiles big. "Never been too good with kids. More of a *enjoy other people's* kind of guy, but I would have done what I could."

"Ronnie, man. I don't even know where to start. *Thanks* is probably a good place—"

"No problem. But if I'm being honest, I did it so I didn't have to take care of those little monsters."

Hooper knows he's kidding but he gets it. Thinks again of how he's been told he's shit with kids.

"Hey, Ronnie." Hooper pulls his wallet. Motions to the cooler. "Need to settle up on the spread here."

"Get me next time, man." Ronnie pops it in reverse.

A thought claps like thunder inside Hooper's mind.

"Wait." Hooper holds up a hand. Ronnie's truck stops.

"You don't have to thank me. It's embarrassing."

"No." Hooper stumbles, finds his balance, then moves closer to the truck. "Don't tell anyone about those kids. I don't really know what's going on and—"

"I know. You told me that too." Ronnie's usually warm expression drifts. "I won't tell a soul. You're right to be careful. There's some wicked souls running around these woods."

"What do you mean?" Looking around, Hooper still can't get over the beauty of this place. Maybe even more so since his little incident at the store.

"I've lived here a long time. Always been some crazies running around here. But in the last, oh I don't know, ten, fifteen or so years, there's been something much worse. Darker, meaner, madder kind of thing."

Hairs on the back of Hooper's neck stand up straight.

"Makes me sad sometimes." Ronnie's eyes fade off, thoughts drifting to a different place. He shakes his head hard, then finds a smile, giving Hooper some of that small-town charm. "Keep them and yourself safe, sir. You hear me?"

Hooper looks down but manages a thumbs-up.

"There's an alarm in there." Ronnie looks for a sign he can try reverse again. "Not a horrible idea to use it."

"Yeah, I don't know how it works."

"There's an emergency code, if I remember right. Real easy. One, two, three... think it goes to six."

Not insanely helpful but it's a start. Hooper nods, waving him off but not wanting him to leave. As the truck backs up and pulls away, his stomach drops. His mind thumbs through everything that's happened in last few hours. Everything Ronnie just said and the look in his eyes as he said it.

Are those wicked souls after the girl and boy?

Scanning the surrounding woods, they look different to him now.

Instead of the beauty he's admired since he's been here, he's now looking between the trees. Hoping he'll spot the danger before it reaches the house. Somehow imagining the woods will hold the line against those dark, mean, and mad things before they get to them.

He balls his fists. The fuzz that coated his mind lifts, replaced by a layer of focus.

Has a reason to zero in on things other than himself or the characters he's created to get him through life.

The front door to the house opens behind him. Can hear her voice before she speaks a syllable.

"Welcome home, dumbass."

The most beautiful poetry he's ever heard.

TWENTY-FIVE

HOOPER SHOVES a fistful of hero pills into his mouth.

Feels Allison's eyes bore through the back of his skull.

She's had this searing, cutting gaze ever since they were kids. Hits his skin like heat coming off a fireball in the sky created by a sibling who wanted melt him into a puddle of goo.

"The hospital, you say? On the floor at the store, you say?" Allison moves back and forth, face red, making quick, whipping turns. The girl and boy watch on. "I don't... What... You can't continue like this."

Hooper stays with her eyes as she lays into him.

"We really, really need to talk about this. No.

Wait. Strike that. You need to listen. I'll talk."
She nudges her head toward the kids. "Do not
drop this on my head. There are some super big,
incredibly bad problems we need to deal with."

She holds open her bag. One that Hooper
knows contains her laptop along with her tablet
and a notebook with feverously scribbled notes.

That bag has shown up at his place in
Manhattan almost every day. Each time, it
contained legal papers, editor's notes, or multiple
other items for mature-minded adults to deal
with.

The struggle within his sister that's raging
right now is not new, he knows. It's in her voice.
It's always been. The layers upon layers of how
she's saying things. A tone tired of the seemingly
never-ending battle, the fight to care without
caring. A war waged to show a lack of caring to
match the firepower of who's cooler than whom
with her brother. It must be exhausting.

He's not hearing the words but feeling what's
being said.

That's in her eyes too. In her shoulders that
have crept up like earrings. However, her eyes
don't match what she's saying, not exactly at
least. Her words fire off like rapid punches, a
series of body blows, setting him up for the big

knockout, but there's a healthy distance behind all that. Way back in the back, there's that caring she probably wishes she didn't possess.

"Allison?" he says in an asking-permission-to-speak tone.

She keeps going.

An engine needing to release its steam before slowing to a stop.

"You're right," Hooper says, hands up in a surrender pose. "You're absolutely right."

Allison stops cold. A record player scratch moment.

The girl and boy stop—their heads were darting back and forth, as if watching some horrible tennis match—look to one another, then turn back to the Hooper and Allison show.

"I'm sorry." Blinking, Allison masks her shock. "Could you repeat that?"

"You. Are. Right. About all of it. The meds. Me. Too many things to list, but you're right and you always have been."

Without thought, without realizing he was doing it, he wraps his arms around her, hugging her tighter than he ever has. He knows this is mostly due to the near-death experience mixed with the chemical whirlwind that's swirling within him, but he doesn't care.

The act of kindness shown by Ronnie more than likely stirred up a little something inside him as well. Hooper would rather not attach labels to everything right now. One of his therapists—he's stopped seeing so many of them—talked about being present, about living in these moments rather than running away from them as fast as he could.

Closing his eyes, sinking into it, he wants to live in this moment for a long time.

He and his sister, there was a time they'd say hello with a hug. They used to be closer. Most of that is on Hooper, though she owns a chunk of the responsibility too. But none of that needs to be hacked up right now. No reason to keep score of battles that have ended, leaving sharp pieces for each of them to use as weapons. No. Not today. Probably not ever.

Allison doesn't hug him back at first. Her arms hang limp by her sides. Hooper imagines shock is still working its way through her. She probably thinks this is some angle he's playing, and in the past, she'd be right to think that.

Then, just as Hooper thinks of letting go, she puts her arms around him.

Light at first, a half-hearted gesture at best—dipping a toe in to test the icy waters—then she squeezes tighter and tighter. Hooper feels the soreness in his back from his little dive at the store as she holds on to him. Robs his breath for a moment, but still, it's pretty great.

Hooper feels thin arms wrap around his legs. Looking down, he sees the boy has hugged their thighs tight together, his face buried, leaving them only the top of his head to see.

Hooper looks over to the girl, who still stands a few feet away, her expression unreadable. Neutral if anything. Not sad or happy. Not frightened or strong. She watches on as if processing behind a dead stare.

Hooper waves to her to come over. Smiles wide, welcoming her to join them.

The girl turns away and leaves the room, walking down the hall.

Hooper's heart falls watching her leave. This perfect moment just shy of perfection. On a certain level he gets it. Even with his boundless imagination, he couldn't even begin to come close to dreaming what's going on in her head.

He hopes Allison found out something, anything, that can help them.

"She's okay." The soft, muffled voice is buried in their legs. "Needs quiet time."

Allison and Hooper pull back, eyes wide in

disbelief. Still only able to see the top of his head. A young boy saying something to a pretty lady is one thing, but this is different. The boy is opening a conversation. Eyes covered, softly spoken, but a massive breakthrough.

"Okay, Hooper?" the boy says, pressing his face into Hooper's leg.

Allison's eyes water as she gives a *well okay, then* shrug.

Hooper lets the tears loose. Couldn't hold them back if he wanted to. Falling, rolling drops that needed to be set free a long time ago. Damn medication.

"Okay, kid."

TWENTY-SIX

GRAVEL CRUNCHES as Ronnie pulls his red truck into the driveway.

Ronnie knows every inch of that house the fancy-pants writer from New York is renting and the others not far from it. The big one Hooper's in, that's the biggest and the fanciest, but all the homes he cares for have their own undeniable charms.

He thinks of them as his children in a way.

In his mind they are special, each with their strengths and weaknesses. Seen them change over that time, worked hard to help deal with the changing seasons, the hard winters, the at times unpredictable spring and fall, then of course the everyday struggles and imperfections time can bring. Helped where he could.

Ronnie's house is a much, much smaller place than the monstrous house Hooper's staying in. A quarter of the size, maybe even less, but it's home. His wife and daughter used to live here with him in this cozy home.

The home that sits at the end of this driveway.

There's a shed in the back where Ronnie does a lot of the extra work that's needed to maintain those properties. The company that manages the ins and outs of the rentals pays him alright money and they've taken care of him over the years. He's never needed much anyway and enjoys the clean air and working with his hands.

Sliding the shift into park, he sees the door to his home is open.

Just a crack.

The wood to the right of lock is splintered, almost completely removed. Ronnie opens his glove box and removes a little .38 he keeps for just such an emergency. In all the years he's lived out here, he's never had a reason to pull it.

Not until now.

His mind thinks of the safe inside the house that holds much more useful firepower. If he can just get to it. Hopes he won't need any of it, but the tingle running along his spine suggests otherwise. Placing his other hand on his cell, he thinks of calling the police.

There's a click of steel locking into steel.

Just behind his ear.

Ronnie's fingers slip away from the phone as the barrel of a gun is pressed to the side of his head. The cold metal held just behind his ear. A terrifying tickle. Turning slow to the left, he sees the police are already here, oddly enough.

Officer Tipton is holding the gun to Ronnie's head.

"Need you to drop that pistol, Ronnie." Tipton's voice is soft and easy but jittery. "Just want to talk."

Ronnie sets the gun down next to him on the truck's long bench seat.

"Really? Talk, huh?" Ronnie isn't sure what this is about, but he's got an idea. "Since when do we need to talk with a gun at my head? Usually talk over coffee."

"Well... yeah."

The front door to the house opens a little wider. Hauk gives him a finger-curl wave.

Ronnie's heart freezes at the sight of him. He's heard that Tipton was under Hauk's thumb but chose not to believe it. Prefers to think the best of people until proven otherwise.

"Might consider shooting me right now, Tipton." Ronnie's teeth grind. "I'm not giving you a damn thing."

"Come on now, Ronnie. All you gotta do is answer the man's questions."

"Don't believe that for a second."

"He just wants to—"

"What's all this about? I haven't done a damn thing to either one of you."

"It's gonna be okay, Ronnie."

"That's so not true and you know it."

Ronnie eyes Tipton. Tipton nods. Yeah, he knows it.

Hauk waves them inside. His thick hand holds a bag of Oreos. Pops one in his mouth and then shakes the bag, as if trying to tempt Ronnie into coming inside for some cookies.

Ronnie eyes the .38 sitting to his right.

Thinks of his options. Thinks about what he knows about Hauk. What he's heard and what he's seen this man do.

Thinks of what Hooper said. Thinks about his new friend and those kids in that big house. It all slides into place. The fear Hooper said those kids had. Ronnie now understands; they're running from the devil himself. His hand crawls ever so slightly toward his gun. So close and yet so damn far.

"Do not do it, man." Tipton presses the barrel of his gun harder into Ronnie's skull.

"What do you want with them?"

"What do you mean?"

"You know damn well." Fights to find some saliva in his mouth. "What'd they ever do to you?"

"That's complicated, Ronnie."

"Always is with you assholes."

Ronnie stares Hauk straight in the eye. Hauk stops chewing his Oreos, shakes his head no. *Don't, Ronnie.*

Ronnie nods yes.

"Officer Tipton," Hauk calls out.

Ronnie twists his head away from Tipton's gun, turning, slamming his body back to the truck's long bench seat. As he twists around, he manages to grab the .38 and squeeze off a wild shot.

The pop booms loud inside the confines of the truck's cab.

Ronnie's ears ring as the bullet zips, cutting into the side of Tipton's face. The shot tears his cheek off the bone, but it could have been much worse. Caught him as he was turning away in defense.

The passenger door behind Ronnie flies open.

Hauk wraps a hand under Ronnie's jaw, the other hand dragging him out of the truck by his hair.

The man moved so fast Ronnie never saw him leave the house's doorway.

He's heard the stories of Hauk. The devil that lives in the woods. Fast. Strong. A heartbeat without mercy or kindness. A dark soul that has just poisoned Ronnie's home.

Ligaments pop, bones crunch as Hauk works to twist the gun free.

Ronnie squeezes off another shot. Hauk snaps his head back left, away from the gun's barrel. The bullet rips the air, sailing out into the blue sky.

"Whoa there, buddy." Hauk stomps his boot down on Ronnie's ribs, giving his wrist a final hard turn.

Ronnie feels the snap.

Bites back the scream. Won't give it to Hauk. Knows he wants it, would like the validation of his pain too much.

Hauk pulls the .38 free from Ronnie's

grasping fingers, tossing it back into the floor-board of the truck.

"Get your shit together," Hauk barks to the other side of the truck.

Tipton holds the side of his face as if it might slide off if he lets go. Sucks in a deep breath, moving around the front of the truck toward Hauk and Ronnie.

"Where are those kids, Ronnie?" Hauk presses his boot down harder into Ronnie's side. "Which house is that Nicholas Hooper hanging out in?"

The pain is unbearable. Like nothing Ronnie has ever felt before. Spots overtake his vision. He sees a faint outline beyond the bright white circles.

Ronnie cracks a grin, blood seeping between his teeth.

"Come on, buddy." Hauk stomps again. "This doesn't have to be this damn hard."

Ronnie sees his daughter step through the bright circles of light that have all but taken over his vision. She smiles. A smile that cuts through it all. The pain. The fear. Through anything Hauk could ever do to him.

She's still young.

Still the age when she passed away with her

mother. He couldn't save her from what happened. Couldn't protect either one of them from the randomness of a drunk driver. He's done everything he can to stay away from any reminders of them. Always working. Rarely sleeping.

"Where? Are?" Hauk alternates his kicks with each word. "Those? Kids?"

Ronnie coughs blood.

"Kids? Hooper?"

Hauk raises his foot up high. Ronnie puts both hands up, grabs the sides of Hauk's boot as his foot comes crashing down. Twisting with all he has left, he catches Hauk off balance and sends him tumbling to the side. Tipton fumbles for his gun while still holding his face.

Ronnie gets up to his feet. His strength at a premium, needs to make it count. Life running on borrowed time.

He plants a shoulder into Tipton, putting him down on the ground. His gun slips from his fingers into the grass. Ronnie picks it up.

A gunshot booms.

A searing heat rips through Ronnie's shoulder. Spins him all the way around.

Hauk lies on his back holding his gun. Pulling the trigger with a jerk, he rips off another shot that zips wide. Ronnie hears the bullet as it passes by. A window to his house shatters behind him. Ronnie pulls the trigger again and again.

Bullets cut up the dirt around Hauk. A tree's bark explodes.

Hauk opens fire. Relentless blasts send Ronnie staggering backwards. Giving everything he has left to stay in the fight. He doesn't even feel his body hit the hard ground. His vision tunnels, thoughts fade.

His wife and daughter whisper kind, soft words.

His smile widens.

I tried.

TWENTY-SEVEN

HOOPER HANDED the boy a popsicle and watched him plop down in front of SpongeBob once again.

He worried for a moment the children were not being provided the proper nutrition that growing girls and boys need while staying at Camp Hooper, but that seems like a secondary issue right now.

Hooper and Allison decided to listen to the boy's advice and give the girl some space. They've moved into the dining room, where they've set up a makeshift command center to try to make some sense of what is going on.

Allison's open bag sits next to her, one of her tablets lit up bright, along with her MacBook Pro and all three of her phones laid out in front them.

There's also an old-school, paper road map that she grabbed at a gas station unfolded across the table, squared creases and all. Hooper didn't realize they still made those things. She's using a fat, yellow highlighter to circle some of the key spots. Positioning the map to the center of the long, hand-crafted table for optimal viewing, suggesting it will give them a good view of the sandbox they're being forced to play in.

Hooper is taken back to how similar this scene is from when they were kids.

Back when they were a much younger brother and sister team, they'd be seated at the family dining room table much like this. Arguing back and forth. Being world-class assholes to one another, some homework being done in-between the verbal kicks and jabs.

Much like now, everything would be laid out across what seemed like the biggest table on this planet or any other. Spiral notebooks, pens and pencils, schoolbooks, along with an encyclopedia or two—usually volume R or M for some reason— and of course a dictionary with some pink *oh shit* erasers at the ready.

Hooper's eyes scan the glass of the screens, taking it all in. Listening to his sister lay out everything for him visually and verbally.

That much has not changed at all. She used to have to boil things down for him even in high school. The content may have been much different back then, but Hooper's highly creative mind has always had problems with details and focus. All the little nitpicky things schools wanted from him didn't seem relevant or interesting in the slightest.

That's where the similarities between then and now end, however.

What's being studied here isn't biology vocabulary words or plotted dates on a Civil War timeline to be memorized and forgotten soon after. This area of study is far more difficult to comprehend. Impossible to forget.

Hooper steals a glance at the boy on the couch, then leans back and looks down the hall. Not sure which room the girl went into, but he knows she's alone. More so than usual. By herself with the weight of the universe pushing down on her tiny shoulders. He swallows, feels his heart break a little more. Ideas of what will become of these children are crushing. Of what has already happened to them too much to consider.

"Hey." Allison snaps her fingers in front of his glossy stare.

She's walking him through what she got from

the detectives and ex-cops they work with. Good old Ross and Dutch being the main sources of intel. They do good work, and are very loyal, but Allison would never let them know what this information was actually for. All her oddly specific questions were under the guise of book research for the genius mind of Nicholas Hooper.

Besides, they're pros, not their first rodeo at all, and they know not to ask questions while only accepting IRS-friendly cash transactions and prepaid debit cards. All above board, sort of, though not long ago Allison did put some healthy deposits into their kids' 529 college funds.

"They did some solid work with this," she says. "Tight turnaround time too."

Amazing work, actually, Hooper thinks.

In no time flat, they uncovered multiple missing persons cases within a fifty-mile radius of this house alone. All within the last thirty days. Way too many missing children in the area over the last sixty days.

Hooper can see his sister's mind attack the data. Pull it apart like a lion digging into the back of an antelope. She hasn't had a chance to process it all, but he can feel her big brain running through the analytics. Can almost hear her mind click like a machine.

She's been driving, talking to Ross, Dutch, and others via Bluetooth in the car, then U-turning, putting the pedal to floor on the way back to this house without having a single true moment to herself to sift through the information they'd dropped on her.

This is her first opportunity to see everything they've sent over to her via encrypted files behind her VPN. Her eyes dance, swiping and soaking up the details.

She's all in now, no question, but Hooper wonders if he did the right thing by pulling her into this. Guilt gnaws at him. He brought her to this house. Of course he had no idea any of this would happen, but still, this was all his big, amazing idea. Rent a big house to write his final masterpiece or die trying.

The very idea stops him.

It's the first time he's admitted it to himself. Sure, he's poked at the edges of the idea. Held it carefully like an egg, so cautious not to break the thin shell. Not wanting to expose what's inside. But this is the first time his mind put it all in one truthful, honest statement.

He came here to die.

Allison continues talking a mile a minute, but he doesn't hear a word.

He's sinking, as if this custom dining room chair was in quicksand. The bulky weight of his decisions pushing him farther down. His fingers spread out on the table, pressing into the wood, trying to create something to hold onto. Scattered words and phrases from his sister land here and there in a staccato style of rat-tat information dump.

No body was found.

Five-year-old missing.

Bruising.

Searching.

Nothing.

What he's heard so far makes Hooper want to curl up in a ball and sob. He's been writing about horrible people doing horrible things for most of his adult life, but this collision of fact and fiction is dragging him under. Hard for him to breathe. He's even holding his breath at times as Allison taps and scrolls through picture after picture. Pinching and expanding text for him to see.

Story after story. Life after life that has ended too soon or been torn to shreds.

He always knew the real world could be far worse than his precious make-believe one, it just never hit him like this before. All the true crime research. The news stories. The documentaries of real-life horror. Never been personal or real to him, always theoretical.

Until now.

Always something horrific that happened to someone he didn't know or care about. Then he'd take that horrible experience, mix it with something from somewhere else, sprinkle in some of his world-class imagination, hit the button on the cerebral blender, then pour it out in witty words on the page.

He was always able to section off the tragic aspect of it in his mind. Keep it boxed up, away from his Peter Pan boyish lifestyle. A *what you don't think about can't hurt you* sort of philosophy... if he'd even taken the time to consider it a philosophy. Quite a trick of compartmentalized denial and ego.

Fingers snap an inch from his nose.

"Hey. Need you firmly in the here and now for this."

Hooper nods. Shakes his head loose from his self-discovery pity party.

"Go." His voice cracks. Punches his thigh hard, forcing himself back online.

Allison moves through the cases, dismissing the ones that don't fit.

Several either don't involve children or only a little girl with no boy. He can see this information is wearing on her too but she's more focused. Let's face it, she's tougher. Forcing herself to stay on the kids she can help. It's not that she doesn't care, it's hitting her as hard or harder than Hooper, but she understands that whole *worry about what you can control* mantra. Whereas Hooper uses his boundless imagination to avoid responsibility for any of it.

He thinks of Johnny Psycho coming for him.

How Mr. Psycho put Hooper on the floor at that grocery. First time they've been introduced formally now that he thinks about it. Johnny Psycho came on quick. Without warning. Hooper was lucky that time. A friend came to his aid. Next time around, he might not live through the meeting.

Silly, silly Hooper.

Will make such a pretty, pretty corpse.

"This one." Allison softly slaps his shoulder, stabbing her finger at the screen.

There's a picture of a modest house with yellow police tape strapped across the front door. Cones have been placed around the front of the house marking various forms of evidence.

"This one. This is the only one that really

makes sense to me. They talked me through it on the phone but now that I'm looking at it..." Allison takes a sip of water, still reading. "The father was shot twice in the sternum and once in the head."

Hooper winces off the photo lighting up the screen.

A man lies dead on the floor. Clean shots perfectly placed just as Allison described.

It's what's behind the pops of blood and flesh that terrify Hooper. Behind the wounds. Beyond the gore. This man, he looks like a nice, ordinary guy. A husband. A father. Some kind soul you went to school with or worked with at some point at some job you both hated.

"Two—" Hooper's words catch in his throat. She hands him her water. "Two kids, I'm guessing."

"Yeah."

"A boy and a girl?"

With a nod, she scrolls down, searches.

"Wait." Hooper takes control of the screen.

Scrolls back up to the picture of the man on the floor. Flips through different angles the police took. There's one he hopes they got.

Holding his breath, he expands one picture in particular with his thumb and finger. Turns to the boy. He's got a perfect view of his profile. He holds the tablet up so he and Allison can compare.

"Little hard to believe they're not related," Hooper whispers.

"No shit." Allison's voice cracks.

She takes the screen from him and scrolls back down, tapping on a new picture. It's a picture of a closet with more police markings for the gathering of ideas to help answer the question of *what the hell happened?*

In his mind, Hooper can see the girl and boy hiding in that closet before she says a single word. Allison tells him they found DNA of the little boy and girl inside the closet. Hooper knows that DNA was probably from their tears.

The burning in his stomach is almost unbearable.

His gift of imagination his worst enemy right now. Where some people wouldn't be able to think of everything, most normal minds couldn't visualize what might have happened in that house, Hooper can see all the possibilities. A punishing, relentless stream of sadness and terror.

"They sat in that closet—" Hooper's knuckles pop as his fists ball.

"Maybe. Look, I know, but don't do this—"

"They heard it all, didn't they?"

"We have to stay focused if we're going to help them. You hear me?"

"They—"

"Listen." She grabs his shoulders, leaning into his face. "I hate what happened to them too. But melting down isn't going to do a damn thing for them. They don't need you to bounce off into space. They need your big brain. You can have your little moment here, that's cool, but when you're done, stuff all that in a box, set it on fire, and get your shit together."

Allison steps away.

Hooper thinks of his breathing. Hard time finding it. She's right. She usually is.

"There's more." She looks out the window. "That text she got. They were able to triangulate some cell towers. The phone that sent it was not far from here. A few miles, actually."

"Close enough for two children to run from there to here."

"Not out of the question. Also, the text itself. The message sent. That tracks too."

He pops his fists open. Wiggles the feeling back into his fingers. Air finds his lungs.

"Their mom being still alive?"

"Yeah. They didn't find her body at the house, or anywhere for that matter. No signs of a sexual assault, but they found a small amount of her blood."

"Was it near the closet?"

"Don't do this."

Hooper grabs the tablet, scrolling and tapping away at the screen like an old typewriter. He finds the picture he saw her move past earlier. A few drops of blood under infrared light. A slight spray a few feet from the closet door. She was going for the closet when they stopped her. She was going to protect her little boy and girl and they took her away.

"Local cops wrote it up as a home invasion." Allison shows him a report on one of her phones. "Drug related."

"What?"

"I know. Sounds like low-grade bullshit."

"There's no way in hell." Hooper swipes back to the picture of the father on the floor. "A pro did this. The wounds. This isn't some tweaker looking for oxy and cash for tacos. Only a stable, trained trigger would put two slugs into a guy's chest with the radius of a baby's fist and then one between the eyes for safety."

"One would think."

Hooper's eyes light up.

"Do you have a picture of the local cop who filed that report?"

Allison opens a new file on the screen and taps. Hooper knows the face before it opens.

"Says it was an Officer Tipton," she says.

Hooper's heart skips a row of beats.

"Guessing you know this clown?"

Hooper nods.

"Let's go talk to the girl." Hooper pushes away from the table. "Show her where that text came from on a map. See if it means anything to—"

There's a knock at the door.

PART THREE

TWENTY-EIGHT

Hᴀᴜᴋ's ᴘʀᴏᴜᴅ ᴏꜰ Tɪᴘᴛᴏɴ.

Took a bullet through the face but still came through.

Of course it included a lot of bitching. Said he didn't know how he was going to hide a bullet wound like that—let alone another dead body—from his police friends, but as Hauk clearly explained that wasn't a Hauk problem. Those were purely Officer Tipton issues.

Still, Hauk has to hand it to Tipton. He actually got this one right. Second try, but he found the right house. At least he's pretty sure.

The first house they checked was clearly not it. There was an elderly man sitting on the porch with his wife, who was in a wheelchair, watching birds and sipping what he guesses was warm tea.

But this massive house?

Hauk has a good gut instinct about things, something he's developed over the years. Credits prison for it mostly. A man can build a sixth sense for what's about to happen while locked up with animals. You kinda have to if your goal is survival. And that funny clawing at the ends of his nerves is leading him to believe this is the place.

Standing amongst the trees, Hauk watches Tipton at the door. Waiting, willing it to open and reveal what he wants to see. Hoping for a visual confirmation that this is it. That he can close the loop on this whole unfortunate mess.

Next to him are two other men.

The Bill brothers. Dollar Bills they call them around here. They each have *The Bills* tattooed on the right side of their neck in a crude prison-style ink. Both share a we'll-do-anything-for-a-few-bucks mentality. Normally, Frakes would be the first call Hauk would make for work like this, but since that's not really an option, he went choice B.

The Bills are men of few words, not incredibly bright, but that is sometimes a blessing in this line of work. Hauk doesn't want or need a mighty mind when the job calls for people to follow direct, simple orders. Hauk wishes Frakes had been more like that at times.

Tipton knocks again. He looks back toward Hauk with a shrug.

"Patience, you stupid bastard," Hauk mutters.

The Bills snicker.

"Don't do a damn thing I don't give the okay to first," Hauk snaps. Knows these boys need clarity. "Got me?"

The Bills nod.

Straighten up their spines. Check their guns, then tuck them behind their backs. Hauk nods, happy they were at least listening to that.

The instructions he gave were straightforward. He told them to use knives, with guns being the *in case of emergency* choice. Gunshots ring out loud around here. If a bullet needs to go, fine, but it shouldn't be the go-to. They have some cover given that Tipton can hold off law enforcement for a while, but still, no reason to announce what's going on here. Of course, the how and why of a big important writer boy going away in the woods?

Well, that is clearly another issue Officer Tipton will need to deal with.

Hauk checks the load on his Glock, tucks it

in the back of his jeans, then pulls a large hunting knife strapped to his leg. Thinks of how easy this should be as he taps the tip with his finger.

Sharp. Good to know.

He presses his finger down with a little more pressure, drawing a dot of red. Thinks of the last time he stabbed someone. The sensation is so different than anything else.

He turns, hearing the door unlock.

"Showtime."

TWENTY-NINE

THE GIRL HEARS Hooper and Allison in the dining room.

They are talking back and forth. She can't make out everything, but it sounds like they are talking about scary things.

She heard Mommy's name.

Then Daddy's.

She sits on the floor in the corner of the game room, her legs pulled up to her chest. Knife gripped tight in her hand. She knows they are trying to help them. Can tell her brother is coming around. Breaking out of his shell, one that he's earned.

She replays those moments in the closet. Minutes and seconds that changed everything. The mean man.

He was arguing with someone. Maybe that scary bald man. She doesn't know, but her body shakes as she thinks about the gunshot. There were three. Then there was screaming. Then there wasn't.

Mommy is still alive.

The mean man sent her that text.

But why? Why would he do that?

She swallows hard. She hasn't cried since all this happened. Not a real cry. Her brother has, almost every night, at least before they got here. Her dad and mom used to tell her she needed to let it all out. That she kept things inside too much. It wasn't good for her.

She thinks about the good cry she'll have when this is over.

There's a knock at the front door.

Her body jolts.

She can feel the air in the house pull tight. Hooper and Allison don't say anything. In her mind, she can see them looking at one another. Maybe whisper-yelling back and forth. She thinks of her brother out there, probably on the couch watching TV.

She gets up from the floor, holding the knife by her side.

To her right are blue skies and trees framed

by the window. The mountains in the distance. The branches sway just bit. She thinks of her and her brother sitting out there only a few nights ago. Maybe it was only one night, she can't remember, but she knows now that the maybe-nice-man in this house is actually pretty nice. So's his sister.

There's another knock.

She leaves the game room, walking with purpose down the hall and into the main part of the house.

Hooper and Allison stand near the door. Hooper is stealing a peek out the side window. They both turn to her. They're worried. Faces all balled up.

"Is it him? The policeman?" she asks.

Hooper manages a nod even though he'd rather not answer the question.

The boy has moved off the couch, taking his place beside his sister. Both resuming their familiar, guarded stances. Just as they were when Hooper opened the door that night. Only this time, that lost, distant look in their eyes is gone. Replaced by something yet to be defined.

She clears her throat. "My name is Emily and his name is Ethan."

Hooper's heart thumps. Allison's jaw drops.

"Hello, Emily and Ethan," Hooper says.

The girl grips the knife in both hands, then softly says...

"Open the door, please."

THIRTY

Hooper places his hand on the doorknob.

He tried to talk the girl, Emily, into putting the knife down.

She refused.

Running out of time, not wanting to upset the progress that's been made, he at least convinced her and her brother to move back into the game room. Safety is a question mark but it was the best place he could think of.

She took the knife in one hand, held her brother's hand in the other, then ran down the hall. Part of Hooper wanted to tell her not to run with the knife, but he realized how dumb that sounded at this stage of the game.

As he sucks in a deep breath, he attempts to clear his pancake batter brain. Remove the clutter. Silence the numbing noise of voices and imagined outcomes soaked in darkness. Shoves it all down by placing one idea in his mind. On his exhale, a singular focus remains, as if the tide has pulled back, revealing a lone gold coin shining in the sun on the beach.

"Protect those damn kids," slips out from his lips. Didn't realize he released it from his thoughts.

Allison bumps her shoulder into his. "Absolutely."

Hooper opens the door.

Office Tipton leans against a column on the porch.

Crooked smile.

Wiry frame accented by a gun that hangs loose on his hip. The side of his face is bandaged with white gauze taped down, a touch of brownish red seeping through.

There's a hint of recognition in Tipton's beady little eyes. A gleam that he's found what he's looking for. Maybe even a sigh of relief. Hooper didn't like this guy before he opened the door. Now, he hates everything about him.

"Yes, officer?" Hooper knows his tone was big, dripping with snark, but doesn't care.

"You Nicholas Hooper?"

272

"I am."

Allison moves into the doorway next to her brother. Tipton's eyes move over to her, scanning her head to toe. Assessing her. Hooper can feel his sister's body tense. Wanting to pounce.

"Is something wrong, Officer..."

"Tipton. Officer Tipton." Taps his badge. "I'm with the local PD here."

Hooper now sees the SUV, police-issued, parked tight behind Allison's car. Pulled in about a foot from their rear bumpers, boxing them in.

Tipton turns, looking behind him. He pauses for what seems like forever. Hooper can't see his face, but Tipton seems to be looking in a particular direction. Hooper can't be sure, but for a moment, he thought he saw a flash of light. Maybe a reflection off something.

Tipton turns back to them.

Was that a signal?

Are there other people in the woods waiting?

Waiting for Tipton to give the green light?

Hooper turns to Allison. She saw it too.

Hooper motions to Tipton's bandaged face. "That looks painful."

"Oh this? Ain't nothing."

"Shaving?"

"Nah."

"Cats, right? You're a cat guy. I like cats."

"Seen any kids around here?" Tipton pushes off the porch's column, moving his feet to shoulder width. Solid stance, squaring his shoulders.

Hooper's blood turns cold.

He knew why this cop is here but now all his gut-churning suspicions have been confirmed. Worst fears at the door. Those kids stood on this same porch. Running away. Looking for safety, for help because of people chasing them. Now they've found them. Johnny Psycho is real, Hooper just got the backstory all wrong.

"Kids?" Hooper asks.

"Yeah, like a little boy and a little girl. Gone missing. Parents are worried sick."

"I bet."

"You can't imagine."

"Bet we can." Allison joins the conversation. "Those kids must be terrified."

"Sure. I'm sure they are. And you are Mrs...."

"Miss go-fuck-yourself."

Hooper coughs, choking on a laugh.

"Whoa now. That's not necessary." Tipton's body goes tight. Face hardens. "Out here trying to help those poor kids."

Hooper spots some movement in the woods just over Tipton's shoulder.

Wasn't much but there's zero doubt there are people back there. Branches move out of time with the wind. A shadow drifts out of place. Every muscle in Hooper's body pulls tight.

A large bald man steps out from the trees, along with two more towering men. Weapons in hand swing by their sides as they walk straight toward the house.

Hooper tries to slam the door shut.

Tipton jams his steel-toe boot inside, wedging it in the bottom of the door. Slaps his hands around the edge of the door, putting his shoulder into it.

Allison kicks with everything she has. Again and again. Tags Tipton in the gut, then the knee. There's a pop. A crack. Tipton grunts as his foot pulls back just enough. Hooper jams the door closed, pinning Tipton's hand.

He can hear the cop's yelp as the door cuts into his flesh.

The door's still open a crack. In his mind, Hooper can see the bald man and his two goons racing hard to get to the door before it closes. Opening the door slightly, Hooper slams it back shut immediately, pushing with all he has until Tipton's fingers release, squeezing outside.

Hooper locks every lock the door has. Wishes there were more.

Allison jumps to the dining room, grabbing a phone. Her fingers shake as the door pounds, thumps as boots try to kick their way in.

She taps in 9-1-1 and puts it on speaker. Digging through her bag, she pulls free a Glock. Her Glock. Hooper watches her sister check the load on the gift she received from Ross and Dutch last Christmas. She paid much more attention during those cop training retreats than he did.

She tosses his gun back to him. The one she took away. Loaded with his one bullet.

"911 what's your emergency?"

Allison picks up the phone, shoving her gun behind her back. Hooper mirrors her move, slipping his gun into the back of his jeans. He knows the 911 response times. Written all about them.

"Call Ross and Dutch next," he yells at her as he runs down the hall toward the game room. "Whatever they can do."

Allison nods.

There's a clink on the glass from the living room.

She whips her head around. A bald man with tats up to his jawline stands at floor-to-ceiling windows gently tapping the handle of his knife on the glass. His grin is huge. Eyes vacant.

The front door is starting to give. She can hear the wood cracking, breaking, hinges will give eventually.

They'll be inside soon.

Getting low, she levels her Glock, taking a position angled at the door. Visualizing mowing them down as they try to breach the door. Another visual punctures her swirling thoughts.

What if she misses?

What if they get to her, get past her, leaving those kids and her brother alone?

Hooper flies down the hall, skidding into the game room. The girl holds her knife steady. Her brother holds a pool cue that's almost as tall as he is.

Good, Hooper thinks. He can hear footsteps rushing through the grass outside. Moving quick around the house.

They'll find a way in one way or another.

Hooper has no idea if all the windows and doors are locked. Allison rushes in, gun raised in one hand, phone in the other.

"Told 911 Officer Tipton is trying to kill us—

she didn't believe me—talked to me like I was crazy—Ross and Dutch are in Newark, can be here in maybe an hour—they're trying some more local people but..."

As her sentence trails off, the pounding at the door continues.

Hooper shakes his head hard.

Think.

Car boxed in. Those men will be on them in no time. They won't make it far, but if they can make it to the woods maybe they can buy themselves some time. No, think about it. Do better. Those assholes know these woods much better than they do. Ronnie talked about the crazies. *There's some wicked souls running around these woods,* he said.

Out of options. They have to fight. Have to find a way to buy time and stay alive.

Turn seconds into minutes. Keep hearts beating.

The four bad guys outside that door are much better at this.

Think.

Allison has a Glock 19. Fifteen rounds. The girl has a knife. The boy a pool cue. Hooper has a gun with one shot. That enough?

Ronnie also said there's an axe downstairs in

the storage. There's an alarm panel by that door. Maybe he can set it off, make some noise, make things loud, draw attention to the place. Maybe he can draw the crazies away from the kids.

Hooper looks around the room. They can't stay in here. They'll be trapped—no exit and one window that doesn't open.

He looks to Allison. "Go upstairs. The master bedroom has multiple ways outside if you need to get out fast."

"Where the hell are you going?"

The front door cracks loud. Time's almost up.

"Meet you up there. Go."

Hooper pushes them along toward the door. They run right, taking the stairs to the second floor two, three at a time. Hooper breaks hard left, legs pumping, heart hammering as he flies down toward the far end of the long hallway.

His feet skid and skip. His hands slap against the wall, doing everything he can to stop himself at the alarm panel. The real estate agent said something about an emergency setting. Ronnie said the code was easy to remember. Closing his eyes, squeezing them tight, he digs into the corners of his mind.

Down the hall, he can hear voices shouting.

"Hoooopeeerrrr," someone chants.

Eyes pop wide. Fingers stab out 1-2-3-4-5-6.

The alarm screams.

An eardrum-shredding wail fills the house. The panel blinks red, pleading for the code that'll tell the alarm company all is well. Hooper allows a satisfied grin as he pushes toward the door leading down into the storage area. As he does, he sees two massive men running into the house. One goes up the stairs to the second floor, the other is headed his way.

"Shit."

Scrambling down the concrete stairs, Hooper's hands fumble, eventually finding the light switch. Boxes on top of boxes. Linens. Things stored here the owner didn't want out in the open, probably. There are some tools along the far wall. Then he finds the axe. Wood handle, big red blade with hints of wear and tear around the edges. Grabbing the axe's handle, he turns.

A thick hand grabs him by the throat.

The alarm is still screaming from above like a wild animal. Drowned out the sounds of this massive wall of meat and muscle coming down the stairs. *The Bills* is tattooed on his neck.

Hooper can see the familiar tunnel in his vision.

No, not now.

The blinding spots of light swallowing up the black hole it surrounds. The sound of the alarm is fading. He feels his grip on the here and now slipping, fumbling away from his mental fingertips.

This man's strength is indescribable. Hooper has never experienced being utterly powerless. Reminds of him hearing the diagnosis. The fluttering moments after. The floating sensation of being helpless punished by the uncontrollable.

Spit flies from his lips as he fights harder than he's ever done his easy life. Remembers why he came to this house in the first place.

He may have come here to die, but not like this.

Hooper angles the axe, turning the blade as much as he can, then raises it just enough and pushes it down into the man's massive thigh. The man's face turns red, fighting the pain, still squeezing tight around Hooper's throat. It's a race to see who gives up first.

Hooper pushes the blade deeper into the man's leg.

Feels the muscles in his back tremble and shake. The man releases Hooper's throat, falling back. Not much, an inch, but enough. Hooper pulls the axe back, gagging to put air back in his lungs, then swings hard like he got a fat pitch. Uses the B of the man's tat as a target. The axe lands into the man's throat.

The man grabs at the axe as Hooper yanks it free. His body slips down onto the concrete floor, where he lies in a pool of his own blood. Hooper fights the urge to throw up, working to shake loose the white blobs in his vision.

Three gunshots ring out.

Sounds like they came from the second floor. Hard to tell from down here. Hooper's head is a mix of soup and fog. The continuing alarm screaming at a high volume. With the axe still held tight in his hand, he drags his body up the stairs.

At the end of the hall stands Officer Tipton with a phone at his ear. Next to him is the tall bald man with tats up to his jaw. The bald man puts up a finger, asking Hooper for a moment, then points to Tipton. *He's on the phone*.

Hooper holds the axe in both hands, moving toward them down the long hallway.

"At the house now." Tipton on the phone, voice dripping with small-town charm. "In the neighborhood when the call went out. A guy named Nicholas Hooper is renting the place, just set it off by mistake. Yeah, that woman you talked to is nuts. Do me a solid and tell the alarm company we're good here." Tipton smiles, still on the phone, bounces his eyebrows at Hooper.

The alarm stops screaming.

Hooper's heart sinks as the silence screams louder than the alarm did. He drops the axe. The bald man shrugs a *sorry, man.*

As the axe clunks to the floor, Hooper pulls his gun from behind him. Using up his one bullet, the shot fires between Tipton and the bald man. Not even close to hitting either one. But that's not the point.

Tipton looks to the bald man.

Hooper can hear someone on the other side of the phone calling out for Tipton. Hooper picks up the axe, smiling back so wide his face hurts.

"Shots fired. Shots fired," Tipton tells the 911 operator. Hates saying the words, but realizes he can't cover that up. Turns to Hauk. "We're fucked."

"How long?" the bald man asks.

"Not long, Hauk."

"Okay." Hauk cocks his head, looking dead at Hooper.

Hauk points up. Tipton runs upstairs.

Hooper runs toward the stairs. Screams until his throat bleeds.

"Allison! Run!"

Hauk pulls his gun free, opening fire.

A white, searing heat rips into Hooper. One bullet tags him in the stomach. Another rips into his shoulder, spinning him to the floor.

Everything goes black.

Flickers of sight come back here and there, off and on. Freezing frames of images blurring into others. As if life had a bad connection.

From the floor, he sees Hauk move up the stairs.

ALLISON HEARS HOOPER scream her name from downstairs.

She puts her hand on the glass door that leads to the deck attached to the master bedroom. Emily and Ethan stand behind her. Emily holds her knife like a torch—both hands extended, locked arms, out in front of her face. Ethan holds the pool cue like a spear. As she begins to open the door, gunshots boom from downstairs. Too many of them.

Hooper only has one bullet.

She bites back a scream. Her brother said to run.

Tipton rounds the corner with his gun raised. He stumbles over the dead body of the other Bill, who's laid out dead on the floor. Three bullet wounds still fresh. Allison opens fire without hesitation. Tipton's body absorbs the multiple blasts, sending him back into the wall.

"Go," she yells to the children, finger pointed out the open door. "Please go right now."

Her gun hand shakes, but is held up tracking the doorway. Tipton slides down the wall to the floor. The children don't require more explanation. They move quick out the door, then climb over the railing of the deck. It's a good drop but nothing they can't handle. There's soft grass beneath.

Ethan jumps.

As Emily readies herself, she hears a voice below. One she's heard before.

"Hey, little girl." Hauk's voice is coated in sick syrup.

She looks over the edge. Down below, Hauk has her brother in his grasp with a gun to his head.

Allison steps behind Emily, her gun pointed at Hauk.

"Hey," Allison calls out, steadying her aim. "Let him—"

"Go!" Emily's body vibrates as the scream tears through the open air.

"Hey now." Hauk's neck cranes up to the deck. "This can all end real easy. No need for a big fuss or more bodies."

A police siren wails in the distance.

Hauk whips his head around. Pulls the gun away from the boy just enough. Allison pulls the trigger. The bullet explodes into Hauk's shoulder. Taking the blast, he spins, firing three quick off-balance shots. Allison drops to the deck, dodging the zipping bullets.

Emily jumps down.

Drops the knife when she lands, but picks it back up and grabs her brother's hand, running full force toward the woods.

Hauk grabs at them as they run by. He's too slow, weakened by his wound, grabbing nothing but air. Pressing his hand to his shoulder, he takes off after them into the woods.

Allison pushes up off the deck. All she can see is Hauk disappearing into the woods, running after the children.

She flies down the stairs, searching left and right for her brother. Finds blood. The sliding glass door is open. Outside, she sees her brother with an axe in hand moving through the grass, hobbling toward the woods.

Running harder than ever, Allison reaches him, throwing his arm over her shoulders, moving them both as fast as they can. Hooper fights through the pain best he can. Fighting for the focus he had earlier.

Protect those kids.

They reach the edge of the woods.

Adrenaline drives back the deep piles of pain. Blood seeps through his fingers as he holds the bullet wound in his stomach. Up ahead, Hauk is closing on the kids. The police sirens are getting closer by the second, but it doesn't matter. They won't be here in time.

"Kill him," Hooper begs Allison.

Allison opens fire. Misses.

Hauk fires back.

A tree's bark explodes next to Hooper's head. Hauk fires again. Hits Allison, putting her on the ground.

Hooper dives for her gun. The earth pops in clumps as the bullets land around him. Hooper's primal scream echoes through the woods as he pulls the trigger, pushing past the white blobs that have all but taken up his vision.

Bullets pop into Hauk, sending him falling into a tree. He hugs the bark tight, holding himself up for a moment before his knees give, then slides down into the dirt.

Emily and Ethan walk up on him. Emily has the knife in her hands, still held like that torch. Her small face in a tight ball of rage.

Hauk coughs hard. Blood webs from his lips as he leans back against the thick tree.

"Frakes was supposed to kill you, kid," Hauk says. "I would have. Can't have live witnesses no matter the age. Might not have enjoyed it, but I would put you both down and then had me a really fine steak. But not Frakes, man. No, he took you both in like little stray pups." Hauk giggles like a small boy.

Emily and Ethan look to each other. Two children trying to process. Trying to understand the words. The idea that the mean man might have had a moment of kindness.

Hooper checks his sister. Allison nods an okay, pointing to Emily and Ethan. Stumbling over, Hooper gets closer to Hauk and the kids, gun in hand.

"You know what's funny as hell? You'll dig this, writer boy. *Irony* I think it is, maybe it's not, who gives a shit. But what's so fun—" He coughs, choking on his escaping life. "We got the wrong house that night."

Emily's eyes go cold. Heart hardens.

"What?" Hooper's question little more than a whisper.

"That's it. A simple little stupid mistake. All this mess that can't be undone, is because that dipshit Tipton got the wrong house. Those kids' folks, they didn't do anything wrong. Just wrong place, wrong damn time."

Emily grips the knife, turns the blade, raises it above her head, taking a step closer to Hauk.

"Isn't that hysterical?"

"Emily," Hooper begs, "put down the knife."

Hauk's laugh is weak but still so loud in their ears.

Ethan puts his hand on her shoulder. They lock eyes. Tears roll down their trembling cheeks. Emily drops the knife. Blade stabs the dirt.

Behind them, back at the house, they can hear car doors open and slam shut. Voices yell and call out.

Hauk slumps to the left. Eyes open but gone.

Hooper puts his arms around the kids as they hold onto him. Their bodies tremble, releasing the cries they've held back for far too long.

Flashes of blue and red lights flicker in the

daylight. Someone shouts about finding blood leading to the woods. Footsteps crunch the grass. Help is close. A helicopter whirls overhead.

Hooper holds the seeping, pulsing wound in his stomach. Might be delusion creeping in but he thought he heard Ross and Dutch back there. Hopes like hell they brought paramedics. Some drugs at least. He imagines the app on his phone —wherever his phone may be—going berserk letting him know he needs to take his hero pills.

Hooper turns back to Allison.

She's pushing herself up on her elbows, back against a tree, covered in sprays and blots of blood. Impossible to tell what's wounds and what's not. She looks to the children, then her gaze shifts to her brother. She extends a slow middle finger to Hooper with 35% of a smile.

Hooper returns the gesture.

EPILOGUE

HOOPER SLIPS in the back with Allison.

They take two seats in the last row. The last two available that are together, but they still have a great view of the stage.

It's a packed house tonight in the Mountain Creek Elementary auditorium.

Well, it doubles as an auditorium. Most of the time it's a place for the children to gather and break noontime bread. The lunch tables are currently folded up and pushed to the side. Dads and moms are still getting settled in waiting for the big show.

They got here late, Hooper's fault, but they are here. Neither one would miss this for anything. Actually, it's not entirely Hooper's fault. There was a flight delay coming into

Denver, but Hooper did indeed screw up the rental car situation. He took his beating on the drive over. The gorgeous view did nothing to keep his sister's verbal assault at bay.

Allison knew she should have handled it.

Regardless, they are here.

The Turkey Tango will be performed this evening—a Thanksgiving tradition at Mountain Creek Elementary—and a little girl named Emily and a boy called Ethan are going to crush this thing.

Their mother told Hooper and Allison all about it a month ago, and Hooper had booked the plane tickets thirty seconds after he hung up the phone. Allison cleared their calendar.

The lights dim, creating the illusion of a big-time theater production. Hooper nudges Allison, pushes his chin toward her bag.

"You do it, ya lazy jackass," she whisper-snaps.

"Come on. You're better at it."

Allison knows he's right, hates defeat no matter what it is. Still, she pulls her phone from her bag and gets ready to shoot a video of the show. Pinching and adjusting the screen to get it just right, she angles to get the best shot of the stage without too much of the crowd.

A mostly bald, portly man parts the reddish curtains. Raising his microphone, he introduces himself as the principal, thanks everyone for coming, and asks that everyone please hold their applause until the end.

Hooper sits up straight.

There are still aches and pains from their time spent with Hauk, the Bills, and Officer Tipton. Scars and lingering effects that may never end. More pills to add to Hooper's diet. Allison has one more surgery, and they both have more healing to do, but they are here now and no amount of bad guys could ever stop that from happening.

Butterflies do battle inside his stomach.

His throat is desert dry. Those kids worked so hard for tonight, he's heard. Been practicing for weeks from what he understands.

Up near the front of the auditorium, Hooper sees the kids' mom looking around the room. Searching for them, no doubt.

They've seen her on the news, and via personal video calls, but it's still staggering how different she looks now. Nothing like when the police found her at that house in the woods. The same house where Emily and Ethan were held in a metal shed. Their mom was in a different shed on the other side of the property the whole time, a hundred yards or less from where the kids were.

Hooper and Allison have heard how the kids struggle with what to do with their feelings about a man named Eddie Frakes. No easy answers. The monster of a man almost ended, then saved, then ultimately altered the course of their lives forever.

Sitting here, all that seems like a lifetime ago.

An old movie showing up every so often while surfing for content.

Hooper puts up a hand, waving toward the mom, trying to be cool while grabbing her attention at the same time. It doesn't work. *Dammit.* Tossing cool aside, he goes with the unbelievably uncool act of standing and waving both arms wildly. Her head turns, spotting the international best-selling author flailing his arms like a proud relative seated at the back of the room.

She smiles wide and warm while giving him a thumbs-up, then crosses her fingers.

Hooper does the same and sits down. They'll all have dinner together after the show at a little place not far from their house. A place the kids love, their mom said. He and Allison will get to hear all about their new school, their new home, new friends, and the boring, absolutely amazing details of their lives.

Hooper and Allison had Ross and Dutch check out the neighborhood, of course. Dug into a couple of the neighbors too. Nothing crazy, they just wanted to know what's what, that's all. *Nice place* was the report back.

The kids are doing okay, at least that's what he and Allison have been told.

Some good days. Some pretty bad.

Therapist said it's a long road, and there will be dark days, but they should grow up to have good, somewhat normal, even happy lives. The most anyone can hope for. They're strong kids. Stronger than Hooper would or could be in their situation. With a fresh start and the right support system, they will be okay. None of it easy, but not impossible either.

The curtains open.

A line of children step out onto the stage. All dressed in brightly colored turkey feathers and sort-of-pointed beaks made of paper with their small upper bodies covered in makeshift brown paper jackets.

A ragtag bunch ready for what the night brings. No matter how much they've prepared, mistakes will be made, but they will keep moving as long as the music keeps playing. Some of the paper on their costumes is ripped, some of it is falling off their shoulders, all of it is perfect.

Parents hold their breath, gasping with glee. Holding their applause as instructed.

The tears flow from Hooper like a mudslide. Allison bites her emotions back, unable to hold the phone steady in the process. Hooper can't help but think how much his friend from the woods would have enjoyed this.

We did okay, Ronnie.

Hooper swallows hard. A moment stabbing into his mind. It all washes over him in a single, crushing wave of everything. The randomness. The untethered events. How little sense can be cut away from any of this.

The news on a Tuesday morning that levels your world.

An unexpected knock at your door.

A simple mistake made by a pack of madmen. A monster that saves.

Someone who picks you up off the floor, buys your groceries. Someone savage that would rather kill everyone and everything.

Traveling across the country to witness the undefinable joy of watching children perform with a room full of strangers. Never knowing. Always changing. Adapt or die.

"Turkey Tango," Hooper whispers.

Elbowing his sister, he points to the stage. In the line, just to the left of the middle, Emily and Ethan look nervous but are buzzing with excitement.

Hooper bites his lip. Nerves along for the ride with them.

He can't take it. Looks to his sister.

She shrugs. Sees it in his eyes. Knows he's about to do something incredibly stupid but that's okay. Plenty of evidence to suggest she'll back him up no matter how stupid things get.

Firing up from his seat, Hooper claps, slow at first, building quick into a thunderous applause. Hands slapping together harder than he's ever clapped for anything ever. Allison lets loose a high-volume whoop.

Some parents eyeball their blatant disobedience of the principal's wishes with self-righteous fire. Other moms and dads simply smile and nod, knowing their story. Knowing all about the woods and everything else and thinking it's wonderful and amazing they are here for those kids. Here in their new village that's welcomed them in.

Hooper finds another gear, clapping even harder. Louder. Stronger.

Allison tears loose a *Hell yeah*.

In two weeks, Hooper will try a procedure in New York. One he told the doctors he'd never agree to just before he left for that humongous house he rented in the woods in order to work his plan.

He's told it has a fifty-two percent success rate. Odds he's more than willing to accept now. Hooper hears that voice in his head. Hasn't heard from his imaginary killer in a while.

Silly, silly Hooper.

Will make such a pretty, pretty corpse.

Emily waves. Ethan waves.

Music starts.

Shut your mouth, Johnny Psycho.

The Turkey Tango begins.

ACKNOWLEDGMENTS

I say the same thing with each book and will continue saying it until it stops being true... you can't do a damn thing alone. So, I'd like to thank the people who gave help and hope during this fun and occasionally nutty writing life.

The list of those people is insanely long. Multiplies by the day actually. And I love them all dearly, so the thought of leaving someone out and listening to them whine and complain later is a little more than I can take on right now.

Fine. I'll point out a couple.

A big thanks to my longtime editor and keeper of the faith, Elizabeth A. White and Christie Hartman for that much needed final look.

Many thanks to the great writers that I'm honored to call friends. You've saved me from giving up on more than one occasion, and without question, I have taken far more than I have given. Hopefully, you know who you are.

Per usual, I can't do any of this without my

roommates. Also known as my amazing family. Words don't cover it.

And finally.

If you're reading this right now, you deserve the biggest thank you of all. Even if we've never met, you've been cool and kind enough to grab a copy of my book and give it a read. That there, my dear, friendly, gorgeous reader deserves one big-ass ACKNOWLEDGEMENT.

Thanks, good people.

If you keep reading. I'll keep writing.

Deal?

ABOUT THE AUTHOR

Mike has been a waiter, securities trader, dishwasher, investment manager, and an unpaid Hollywood intern. He's quit corporate America, come back, been fired, been promoted, been fired, and currently, from his home in Texas, he writes stories about questionable people making questionable decisions.

Keep up with Mike at...
www.mikemccrary.com
mccrarynews@mikemccrary.com